KU-531-077

THE BABY THE BILLIONAIRE DEMANDS

JENNIE LUCAS

MIX
Paper from
responsible sources
FSC
FSC C007454

s book is produced from independently certified FSC™ pa
to ensure responsible forest management.
For more information visit: www.harpercollins.co.uk/green.

Printed and bound in Spain
by CPI, Barcelona

MILLS & BOON

All rights reserved including the right of reproduction
in whole or in part in any form. This edition is published
by arrangement with Harlequin Books S.A.

This is a work of fiction. Names, characters, places, locations
and incidents are purely fictional and bear no relationship to
any real life individuals, living or dead, or to any actual places,
business establishments, locations, events or incidents.
Any resemblance is entirely coincidental.

This book is sold subject to the condition that it shall not,
by way of trade or otherwise, be lent, resold, hired out
or otherwise circulated without the prior consent of the publisher
in any form of binding or cover other than that in which it is published
and without a similar condition including this condition
being imposed on the subsequent purchaser.

® and TM are trademarks owned and used by the trademark owner
and/or its licensee. Trademarks marked with ® are registered with the
United Kingdom Patent Office and/or the Office for Harmonisation
in the Internal Market and in other countries.

First Published in Great Britain 2018
by Mills & Boon, an imprint of HarperCollins*Publishers*
1 London Bridge Street, London, SE1 9GF

© 2018 Jennie Lucas

ISBN: 978-0-263-93498-4

This _____ per

F

MORAY COUNCIL LIBRARIES & INFO.SERVICES	
20 45 56 50	
Askews & Holts	
RF	

Dear Reader,

Which is more important—love or money?

After a difficult childhood, Lola Price knows the answer: *Money.* Having lost her family to tragedy and poverty, she has vowed that now she's grown up she'll have so much money she'll never feel helpless again.

At twenty-four, Lola falls in love with her boss, Spanish media mogul Rodrigo Cabrera. After a hot affair she's thrilled to discover she's pregnant—until Rodrigo finds out about her shocking past and coldly tosses her from his house.

Heartbroken, Lola flees to New York without telling him about the baby. As much as he now despises her, she's afraid the ruthless billionaire might try to take her child away.

What will happen when Rodrigo finally learns her secret?

Which will triumph—love or money?

This is the final book in a trilogy about three friends. Hallie's story was *The Secret the Italian Claims.* Tess's was *The Heir the Prince Secures.* I've loved writing these stories about three vibrant, different women and their fiercely powerful men. I hope you love them too.

With warmest wishes,

Jennie

CHAPTER ONE

MONEY MEANT EVERYTHING to Lola Price.

Money was the difference between happiness and grief. Between joy and tragedy. She'd learned it at five years old, and every day since.

Growing up in a trailer on the edge of the California desert, in a dusty town where jobs were scarce, she'd seen her mother's daily struggles to pay the bills after Lola's father died. Her mother eventually remarried, but it only made things worse.

By the time she was eighteen, Lola had learned that there was only one way to protect the people you loved. One way to keep them safe and close—and alive.

You had to be rich.

So she'd dropped out of high school and moved to Los Angeles. Desperate to save what was left of her family— and without any talent or even a high school diploma— she'd hoped to instantly become a movie star, but her acting career never got off the ground. Without money, she'd lost everything.

Now she had a four-month-old son. And nearly a million dollars. Lola took a deep breath. No one would ever take her family from her again.

Sergei Morozov's booming voice brought her back to the charity ball, where he'd been swaying with her on the dance floor. "Can I kiss you, *Lolitchka*?"

"What?" Startled, Lola looked up at him. "Kiss me?"

"Yes. When?"

"Um…never?"

The Russian tycoon winced. Burly and in his mid-fifties, with gray hair on his temples and a strong accent, he was CEO of a large Wall Street firm. He'd also been, until four months ago, her employer. "When you agreed to be my date tonight, I thought…"

"I'm sorry. I don't feel that way about you." Around them, couples danced in the gilded hotel ballroom to the orchestra's elegant music. The children's charity ball was the social occasion of November in New York. She was just surprised her two best friends, Hallie and Tess, both newly married to billionaires, weren't here. They loved fancy events like this.

But Lola didn't see them. As she danced with her former boss—keeping an old-fashioned, almost Victorian distance between them—she saw dark-haired men everywhere in sleek, sophisticated tuxedos who reminded her of another previous boss, Rodrigo Cabrera. The Spanish media tycoon who'd coldly given her a million-dollar check, then tossed her out of his beach house, secretly pregnant and brokenhearted.

Sergei cleared his throat. "If you just need a little more time…"

"That's not it." She looked down at the marble ballroom floor. She never should have agreed to a date, she thought. She'd been swayed by her neighbor, a widow who occasionally babysat her son, who'd told Lola she 'needed to get out and live.' That, plus the weddings of Lola's two best friends in rapid succession, had made her feel her own loneliness. When Sergei Morozov had invited her out, she'd convinced herself it might be a healthy step forward, after a hard, lonely year.

Now she wished she'd just stayed at home.

"Some man broke your heart," he growled. "He abandoned you and your son."

Lola looked up in astonishment. She'd never spoken about Rodrigo to anyone, not even her best friends. "I never said he abandoned me—"

"You had pregnancy alone. Had birth alone. No man." His big hands tightened against her back. "Forget the idea of a date. Maybe I just marry you, eh?"

She sucked in her breath. "Marry?"

The burly man looked down at her. "I have wanted you for a long time, Lola," he said softly. "If marriage is your price, I am willing to pay."

Lola stared up at him in shock.

Marry him?

Her stomach looped like a roller-coaster.

Sergei Morozov wasn't a bad man. She'd worked as his secretary throughout her pregnancy. He was rich, arrogant, but not cruel. When she was eighteen, she would have jumped at the chance to marry a man like that.

Too bad for him that Lola was now twenty-five, with a pocketful of money and a scarred, bitter heart.

"I'm flattered, truly," she said awkwardly, "but—"

"Marry me, *zvezda moya*. I will cover you with jewels. I will—"

"I'd like to cut in."

Lola's heart dropped as she heard another man's voice, low and dangerous behind her. A voice she knew, though she hadn't heard it in over a year. A voice she'd never forget.

Slowly, she turned.

Rodrigo Cabrera stood beside her on the dance floor, wearing a sleek tuxedo over his muscular, powerful body.

Dark-haired, dark-eyed, with chiseled cheekbones and a five o'clock shadow along the hard, sharp edge of his jaw, he was even more handsome than she remembered.

Power, dark and dangerous and sexy, echoed off him like shock waves.

"Rodrigo?" she breathed.

"Lola." His cruel, sensual lips curved as he looked down at her. "It's been a long time."

Unwilling images went through her of the days and nights of their brief affair. The pleasure. The joy. The laughter. The certainty in Lola that for the first time since she could remember, she was no longer alone...

Now, pain twisted through her, pain she was careful not to reveal on her face. "What are you doing here?"

"Cutting in." He moved between her and Sergei with almost feline grace. He glanced at the Russian tycoon with casual amusement. "If you don't mind."

Sergei scowled. "Of course I mind—"

"It's all right, Sergei." Lola put her hand unsteadily on his arm. "I'll see you shortly."

Sergei set his jaw. "Once the dance is done, I'll be back."

Rodrigo's eyes flicked to her. "As the lady pleases."

After Sergei's grudging departure, the two of them looked at each other.

"So you're living in New York now," Rodrigo said coldly. "Are you here on business?"

He bared his teeth into a smile. "Is there any other reason?"

In spite of everything, Lola's heart was in her throat as she looked up at him. All the other people in the ballroom, all the laughter and music, faded away.

Slowly, Rodrigo pulled her into his arms. She breathed in his scent, of woodsy musk and soap and something uniquely him. She tried to tell herself she felt nothing, but her knees trembled, and she was glad he was supporting her in the dance.

He glanced back at Sergei, now glowering at them from the edge of the dance floor. "So he wants to marry you."

"Not everyone hates marriage like you do," she said unwillingly.

His lips quirked. "Another millionaire falls at your feet."

"Not everyone hates *me* like you do."

"I don't hate you, Lola." His voice was low.

She tilted her head back to look at him beneath her lashes. "You don't?"

"I despise you. That's different." His dark eyes gleamed. "You must have spent the million dollars I gave you if you're looking for a new sugar daddy. Do you intend to say yes? Are congratulations in order?"

Lola narrowed her eyes. She wondered what Rodrigo would say if he knew the real reason she'd taken his payoff money: because she'd found out she was pregnant.

Money meant more to her than pride. It meant safety. Her baby must never know, as Lola once had, how it felt to go hungry. He must never see his mother cry when she couldn't pay the bills, or be mocked for wearing clothes to school that were too small, or harassed by teachers for falling asleep in class, because he'd spent another night taking care of younger siblings when his mother had the night shift.

And most of all: Jett must never know how it felt to lose his family.

Taking Rodrigo's money meant no one would be able to take her baby away from her.

No one, that was, except Rodrigo.

She swallowed, her hands tightening on the shoulders of his tuxedo jacket as they danced. A father had rights. And although she still had most of the million dollars that he'd given her, she knew he had billions more. Enough to take whatever he wanted. Even Jett. And that made her afraid.

Because she'd been his secretary once. For over two years before they'd become lovers. She knew how ruthless the Spanish media mogul could be. How he could turn on people savagely if they failed him.

Rodrigo had good reason to believe the worst of her. Why wouldn't he, after what he'd learned about her past?

But he was in New York on business. He often came here. He even owned a house in SoHo. But they traveled in different circles now. He couldn't know about Jett.

If he did…

No. He must never know.

Rodrigo's expression hardened. "Well? Do you intend to marry him?"

"I haven't decided," she mumbled.

His arms tightened around her waist. "Is that a lie?"

Lola had no intention of going on another date with Sergei, let alone marrying him. But she wasn't going to tell him that. She looked up. "Why do you care?"

His dark eyes glinted. "I don't. I'm just wondering if I should warn him about the kind of woman you really are."

She stiffened. "What kind is that?"

"You're very beautiful, Lola." Rodrigo's hot gaze traced slowly over her modest, long-sleeved black knit dress. As they danced to the music, he cupped her cheek. *"Very."*

Electricity ripped through her body from where he'd touched her. Sparks raced down her spine, shouting, *Yes, yes.* This was her man, and she'd missed him, oh, how she'd missed him. She'd dreamed of him unwillingly every night from the moment he'd taken her virginity and made her feel—

Rodrigo dropped his hand. "But you're ugly on the inside. You'll do anything for money. Anything? *Anyone.*"

His cruel words were like a blow.

With a deep breath, she cut off the connection between her heart and her brain. She didn't care if he insulted her, she told herself. She just had to get through this song. Then he'd leave. And she'd make sure she never saw Rodrigo Cabrera again, or put Jett at risk of being taken from her.

Lola tilted her head, looking at him sardonically. "Ah. There's your famous charm. If you think I'm so horrible, why don't you go dance with someone else?"

"Why? Are you so eager to be back in your lover's arms?"

As if she'd ever let Sergei caress her! As the song finally drew to a close, she stopped dancing, nearly trembling with relief. "Okay, song's over. Not that this wasn't fun, but— well, it wasn't. Go find some other woman to torture."

Rodrigo stopped, looking down at her on the dance floor.

"And that's all you have to say to me?" he said softly. "After a year?"

Their eyes locked, and for a moment, in spite of her overwhelming fear, the truth rose guiltily to her throat. Once, they'd been so close; once, she'd told him everything.

No. She hadn't told him everything. And that had been what had destroyed them.

A hulking shadow appeared beside her. "Song is over," Sergei said sullenly. "I'm taking her back."

Lola looked at the Russian with gratitude, then glanced one last time at the Spaniard she'd once loved with all her heart. "I guess this is goodbye."

"I guess so," Rodrigo said, his dark eyes unreadable. He turned away.

The orchestra started a new song, and couples resumed swirling around them on the dance floor. Lola turned to Sergei. "I'm tired," she choked out. "Will you please take me home?"

"Konyechna." Sergei's voice was soothing. "I'm sure you miss your baby."

Lola sucked in her breath, praying Rodrigo hadn't heard. No such luck. As if in slow motion, he turned back to her.

"Baby?"

"Nothing to do with you." But her voice was strained, even to her own ears. She had to get out of here—fast. Tossing her blond hair as if she didn't have a care in the world, she turned back to Sergei. "Let's go…"

But Rodrigo blocked her path. "How old is the baby?"

"None of your business."

As she tried to walk past him, Rodrigo grabbed her wrist. His black eyes glittered. "How old, damn you?"

"It doesn't matter!" She struggled, desperately trying to hide her fear. "He's not yours!"

But as Lola croaked out the lie, her cheeks went red-hot. There was a reason she'd been such a washout as an actress. She was the worst liar in the world.

Searching her gaze, Rodrigo's eyes suddenly widened. Dropping her wrist, he staggered back.

He knew. She hadn't told him, but he still knew.

The ballroom started spinning around her. She tried to think of some way to get out of this. But her brain was frozen.

"The baby's mine," Rodrigo said in a low voice. "Isn't it?"

"Don't be ridiculous," she snapped. She pointed at Sergei. "He's the father."

She desperately hoped the Russian tycoon would play along. But Sergei just looked bewildered.

Rodrigo swept him with a dismissive glance, then faced Lola. His cold expression turned to fire as his dark eyes glittered in the light of the ballroom.

"Tell me the truth," he said in a low, dangerous voice. He gripped her shoulder. "I want to hear you say it."

"Let me go," she whispered, her throat closing.

All her fears were crashing around her like bricks. Lola tried to lift her chin, to glare at him, to defy him. Most of all, she tried to think of a good lie.

But looking up at Rodrigo's hard, handsome face, she

knew it would be no good. When it came to him, her lies always betrayed her.

"Tell me, Lola," he demanded mercilessly.

Heart pounding, she whispered, "Yes. You're the father."

A baby.

Rodrigo staggered back.

She'd had his baby.

The shock of that idea swirled in his brain, leaving him staring down at Lola in confusion.

From the moment Rodrigo had arrived tonight at the charity ball, coming alone as he couldn't be bothered to choose a date, he'd been the center of attention on the red carpet, not just from paparazzi, but from the other guests. As a wealthy, powerful billionaire, he could build anyone's movie career instantly across his entertainment empire. Rodrigo was eagerly greeted by famous actors and directors and beautiful women who all wanted a piece of him.

He barely paid attention. He was used to it; bored by it. He didn't fool himself that these women were after anything but his body, his money or his power. They weren't interested in him personally.

As a younger man, he'd relished the notice he received from beautiful women. But he'd been desperate then to find love, to get married, to have a home. How else to explain why he'd proposed to three different women in his younger years?

Remembering that disgusted him now. Humiliated him.

Love was for the naive. Only fools believed in a communion of souls. Men, as a rule, weren't supposed to yearn for such things.

But he once had. Stupidly.

Rodrigo was monogamous by nature. That was his darkest secret. He'd been the only child of wealthy, neglectful parents. Growing up, he'd dreamed of having a loving family and home. Even after he'd first taken over his father's small film studio in Madrid, he'd wanted some version of the fairy tales he manufactured for a living.

Ridiculous to think of it now. Because he'd swiftly learned his lesson. All three fiancées had cheated on him before the wedding date.

He'd never proposed to Lola Price, of course. He'd never even let himself love her during their brief affair. He was no longer that stupid, or that young, to believe in dreams of love and forever.

But he'd known her. Trusted her. She'd been his assistant for years before she'd been his lover. Working together, day in and day out, he'd been impressed by her determination, intelligence and drive. He'd respected her. Admired her.

But he hadn't touched her, in spite of her incredible beauty. He'd valued her far too much as his assistant to wreck everything for a brief affair, which was all it could surely be.

Until, one night in Mexico City, after they'd closed a deal, they'd celebrated with too much tequila at a famous restaurant. Then Lola had suddenly leaned over the table and kissed him.

It had been a revelation. An explosion.

They'd had a few incredible months, working together by day, making love by night. It had been—perfect.

Then Rodrigo had learned who Lola really was, deep down. What she'd done when she was eighteen. And that she'd been playing him all along. She'd claimed to love him. But all she'd ever wanted was his money.

He'd been stupidly blind. That was what hurt his pride the most. He'd let himself believe she actually cared. He would never forgive her for that. Or himself…

For the last year, he'd avoided thinking about her. He'd tried to forget. He'd told himself that he had.

Then he'd seen her on the dance floor tonight, in the arms of another man.

Lola.

She'd looked even more dazzling than he remembered, her hazel eyes huge in her beautiful face, her hips swaying in a slinky dress that fit her slender, curvaceous body like a glove. For a moment, when he first saw her, Rodrigo's heart had twisted.

Then he'd remembered how she'd deceived him, and taken the million-dollar check he'd thrown in her face in his fury. Cold rage had filled every space in his heart, leaving no room for any other emotion.

Lola Price had no shame. She was a liar, a deceitful gold digger. But he'd never imagined that even she could try something like hiding a pregnancy. Stealing his child away.

Rodrigo's arms tightened as he looked down at her.

She'd lost the tan she'd had in California. Her skin was pale, and she was dressed in head-to-toe black, like a true New Yorker. The knit dress had long sleeves, a high neckline and a hem to the floor. The only skin showing was her face and her hands.

It shouldn't have been sexy, but it was.

Everywhere he looked, Rodrigo saw something to tempt him, from the shocking beauty of her perfect face, with her high cheekbones, changeable hazel eyes and bee-stung lips, to her long, elegant throat. Even her hands drew him, with their graceful tapering fingers.

As his assistant, Lola had always been well-groomed and professional, as befitted the powerful executive assistant of an entertainment mogul. Now, he saw her beauty and wondered if she was trying to lure the burly, gray-haired Russian scowling beside her. Who was he? Her lover? Her soon-to-be husband?

The thought made him sick.

As the CEO of Cabrera Media Group, an international

entertainment conglomerate, Rodrigo was surrounded by beautiful women on a regular basis. His companies produced films and TV series around the world. He owned studios and networks and was about to launch a new streaming media company in South America. He should have been immune to Lola Price's charms.

But he wasn't. He still wanted her. Now more than ever. Maybe that was why, for the last year, he hadn't been able to touch another woman.

After a year of hot, frustrated need, no wonder his whole body felt the effect of being close to Lola now. Even as he learned of her latest betrayal.

Damn her.

"You were pregnant when you left California," he said in a low, dangerous voice. "And you never told me."

The sparkling lights of the chandeliers, soaring high above in the hotel ballroom, seemed to leave shadows across her beautiful face as couples continued to move around them on the dance floor.

Only the three of them did not move. The burly Russian turned to Lola in shock. "This is your baby's father? This man?"

She looked pale. "I think you should go, Sergei."

The man glanced uncomfortably toward Rodrigo. "If you would like me to stay, *Lolitchka*, if you need help—"

"No, thank you," she whispered. "It's better I do this alone."

"You heard what she said," Rodrigo bit out. "Get the hell away from her."

The older man's eyes narrowed, but he just turned to kiss Lola's cheek. "If you need me, I am always here."

The grateful look she threw Sergei made Rodrigo suddenly want to bash his face in. His hands tightened into fists at his sides until the other man left.

Taking Lola's hand, Rodrigo grimly pulled her away

from the crowds. He tried not to notice how soft her palm felt against his. He tried not to feel the electricity that pulsed through his body at that innocent touch.

In a darkened, empty corner of the ballroom, he turned to face her accusingly. "How could you not tell me?"

Lola wouldn't meet his eyes. "Because I don't need anything from you. I don't want anything."

I want you, Rodrigo. The memory went through him of the trembling ecstasy of her voice, long ago. *And I... I love you.*

As he looked down at her beautiful face, shadowed by the chandelier's light, he felt a rush of unwilling emotion as he remembered when she'd first spoken those words.

Two months into their affair, after closing a big business deal in Los Angeles, they'd returned to his beach house in triumph. Drinking wine, they'd lingered at midnight alone on his private beach, around a small bonfire he'd built from driftwood as the moonlight floated down. He could still smell the salt of the sea and vanilla fragrance of her hair as the hot Santa Ana winds blew against their overheated skin. He could hear the crackling of the fire and the roar of the waves when Lola had told him, her voice breathless and trembling, that she loved him.

For an answer, he'd kissed her, drawing her down against the soft blanket on the sand. In that moment, he'd been half out of his mind. In that moment, he'd almost wanted to love her back—

But Rodrigo didn't want to think of that, or the intensity of the grief and betrayal he'd felt a month later, when he'd learned the truth about her past from Marnie, his longest-serving, most loyal employee.

Sir, Marnie had said sadly. *Sir, there's something you should know about Lola Price—*

New anger went through him, pouring over his grief

and regret. But even that could not block out his biggest emotion.

Desire.

Even now, with his heart pounding with rage, he wanted her. His hands shook with the effort of not grabbing her and wrenching her into his arms for a kiss. His blood was boiling with the need to take her. To push her against the wall—to kiss her—to make her want him as badly as he wanted her, and make her regret—

Taking a deep breath, Rodrigo narrowed his eyes. "How could you keep my child secret? I never thought even you could sink so low."

Lola's cheeks turned white, then red. "I was going to tell you I was pregnant the night you threw me out. But you stopped me—remember?"

Rodrigo did remember that awful night, how she'd shown up at his beach house with joy in her eyes.

I have something to tell you—

Me first, he'd said flatly. *I saw the pictures. I know what you did.* He'd looked over her scornfully. *I know who you are.*

Lola's beautiful face had fallen, her expression suddenly tortured and guilty. Uncharacteristically for her, she hadn't tried to argue or fight. She'd just accepted his accusations with slumped shoulders. Until, finally, trying to get a re-action out of her, he'd written out the million-dollar check and tossed it in her face.

That's what you've wanted, isn't it? You were tired of being my assistant and hoped to upgrade your position to be my mistress or, better yet, wife! If money is what you want, here—take it!

Rodrigo had waited, heart pounding, for her to explain. He'd waited for her to throw the check back in his face. He could have forgiven her past. No one was perfect. Certainly he was not. What he couldn't forgive was her deliberately playing him for a fool, convincing him that she loved him, when all along she'd only had her eye on his wallet.

With a bowed head, she'd looked down at the million-dollar check. Then she'd crushed it in her hand, and left the beach house without a word. And he'd known his worst fears about her were true.

"You lied to me," Rodrigo said coldly now. "You moved three thousand miles away to keep your pregnancy a secret."

"You clearly didn't care about me." Her hazel eyes glittered. "So why would I think you'd care about our child?"

"It wasn't for the baby's sake. You did it to punish me."

Lola lifted her chin. The cold rage in her expression matched his own.

"You fired me. Tossed me out of your house. Told me you never wanted to see me again. You called me names and threw a check in my face. Why would I ever tell you I was pregnant?"

"So you stole my child away from me. Like a thief in the night."

She lifted her eyes furiously. "You made it clear you hated me. Why would I want to give you rights over my baby?"

Rodrigo refused to concede her the slightest bit of sympathy. Lola was a greedy, coldhearted gold digger. Hadn't she proved that, when she'd taken the check?

But she'd taken the check to provide for their child.

Suddenly, he sucked in his breath.

She'd known she was pregnant when she left. If she'd really been a gold digger, she wouldn't have simply taken his money and disappeared from California. No.

She would have told him about the pregnancy immediately, knowing that, as mother to Rodrigo's only child, she could have gotten far, far more than a mere million dollars.

But she hadn't.

Had he been…wrong about her?

He pushed down the emotion rising in his heart. No. He couldn't believe that. He clenched his jaw.

"So you moved to New York and replaced me with another rich man."

Lola shook her head. "Sergei was just my boss. I worked for him during my pregnancy, until the baby was born."

He frowned. "You worked?"

"As his secretary."

He wasn't surprised Lola had easily found a new job. She'd been a stellar assistant, and after their breakup, when he'd fired her, he'd still directed his HR staff to give her the glowing reference her work deserved. But, he didn't understand. "Why would you work? You had my check."

She lifted her chin. "I've kept that money in reserve to provide for the baby. I got us a nice apartment, and have stayed home since he was born, to take care of him. And—" she mumbled, looking away "—I studied for my GED."

Rodrigo stared at her in shock. "Your what?"

Lola looked at him. "It means General Equivalency Diploma—"

"I know what it means," he snapped at her. "But why would you need one?"

"Employers expect at least a high school diploma these days, if not a college degree. I was tired of feeling bad about it. So I studied for the test." She bit her lip. "I took it last week. I haven't heard yet if I passed."

"You're worrying about your résumé?" Jealousy pulsed through him, unwelcome and unreasonable. "That Russian was offering to marry you and cover you with diamonds."

Lola's lips lifted bitterly. "I loved one rich man, once." Her voice was acid. "That experience was enough for a lifetime. My son and I are better off alone."

Rodrigo's world was spinning. "Son? What's his name?"

"Jett. Jett Price."

He blinked. "You called him what?"

"What's wrong with it?" she said defensively.

"It sounds like something that might get mentioned in a stock report from Boeing or Airbus. Jet price?"

"No one will think of it that way!"

"His surname should be Cabrera."

She lifted her chin defiantly. "He's fine as he is."

"I want a paternity test. And then—"

"Then what?"

"Then we'll see," he said softly.

Lola looked at him for a long moment. Most of the people in his world feared him, and with good reason. He'd built his media empire by being ruthless and unpredictable. Looking down at her, he half expected to see fear. He should have known better.

"We're better off without you." Her eyes were defiant. "I won't let you take my child from me, Rodrigo."

"And you think you can fight me?" he said softly. "You know what I'm capable of."

"Yes." Lola lifted her chin. "And you know me."

"What does that mean?"

"If you try to take my son from me, you'll regret it."

He looked at her incredulously. "You're threatening me?"

She lifted an eyebrow. "It's a promise."

"And how would you fight me?"

"I've made some powerful friends."

Her eyes were cold. Rodrigo thought of her date. Sergei was obviously wealthy, and he'd proposed marriage. Was that the powerful friend she meant?

She'd said she was his secretary. That she'd refused his proposal. But for all he knew, they were lovers. The image came to him of her naked in the man's arms. The thought made him sick.

Rodrigo had been Lola's first lover. Of that, there could be no doubt. When they'd first made love, and he'd discovered her virginity, he'd been shocked, exhilarated, intoxicated with pride. Lola, so beautiful and desirable, had somehow still been a virgin at twenty-four.

But she might well have taken lovers since then. Any man would want her. While Rodrigo had been celibate as a monk.

"You and that Russian," he said with deliberate carelessness, "you are lovers, of course."

Her lips twisted. "I've never even let him kiss me."

He stared at her. No. It couldn't be true. Blinking hard, Rodrigo regained his reason. All the time she'd worked for him, he'd thought she was a terrible liar. But he must have been mistaken. Of course she was sleeping with the other man. Why else would he propose? What a little actress she was. Really, he should hire her for his next prestige film. "Liar."

"I'm not," she bit out, her eyes flashing. "I've only kissed one person in my whole life—"

She cut off her words, but it was too late. He stared at her, his heart twisting violently in his chest.

"You've never kissed another man? Even now?" He came closer. "Even after all this time?"

She looked up at him, her eyes shooting sparks. "I loved you, Rodrigo. Do you even know what that means? No. You don't. How could you, when you felt nothing?"

A razorblade lifted to his throat. He tried to keep his grip on reason. He ground out his words. "Why would the man propose, if he's never even slept with you?"

Her hazel eyes were luminous in the shadows of the ballroom. "Because he thinks it's the only way he can have me."

For a moment, Rodrigo couldn't breathe. Suddenly, it was as if a veil had been lifted from his eyes. He'd been right all those years he'd thought she wasn't a good liar. She wasn't. He could always tell on those rare occasions when she tried to lie. Her voice got strangled, her face turned red. He knew when she was speaking the truth.

And he could hear the truth in her voice when she said she'd loved him.

Had he been wrong about her all this time?

He wasn't wrong about one thing, at least, he told himself fiercely. He wasn't wrong about her stealing his child away.

"I want to see the baby," he said tightly.

"Now?"

"Now."

"Fine," Lola said coldly. "I'll get my coat. You can meet him. But that's it."

As he followed her out of the hotel ballroom, Rodrigo's gaze slowly traced down her body. Her generous breasts were even fuller than he remembered, emphasizing her hourglass curves, her tiny waist and perfect hips. She wore no jewelry. She didn't need jewels. Not when her eyes sparkled in her beautiful face. Not when she had that body. No man in the room could take his eyes off her—and Rodrigo was no exception.

Damn her.

His jaw tensed as he remembered the angry tremble of her voice. *We're better off without you.*

It wasn't true, he thought. He stiffened, remembering his own father. He was nothing like that bastard.

Maybe he didn't know much about fatherhood or parenting or happy families, but he could at least give his son a name. A stable home. A good childhood.

He could give him everything he himself had never had.

His eyes fell on Lola. Whether she liked it or not, Rodrigo was the one in control now. His eyes traced the full curve of her backside, the span of her tiny waist.

And he intended to have his way. At any cost.

CHAPTER TWO

LOLA WAS IN SHOCK.

Gripping her arm, Rodrigo led her out of the ballroom and helped her collect her coat—a black faux fur—then led her out of the grand hotel. He handed his ticket to the valet, who brought his Ferrari around, gleaming sleekly in the night.

Now, it was just the two of them, alone in his car.

Lola tapped her high heel nervously in the passenger seat as he drove. She glanced at him out of the corner of her eye.

Maybe it was all for the best that he'd found out, she tried to convince herself. She hated lying, mostly because she was so bad at it. At least now it was all in the open.

She hadn't lied when she'd said she had powerful friends who would help her. Her two best friends were both married to billionaires, Hallie Moretti to the owner of the luxury Campania hotels, and Princess Tess Zacco di Gioreale to a Sicilian prince. Tess was also now a fashion designer in her own right. Lola had had to sneak out of Tess's first fashion show last week in order to secretly take the evening GED test. She didn't want her friends to know about it. Not until she knew she'd passed.

Lola hated admitting weakness of any kind. Which was why she'd never told her best friends anything about Jett's father.

But if Rodrigo tried to take custody, she knew her

friends would do anything for her—and their ruthless, adoring husbands would do anything for *them*.

She wouldn't let anyone take Jett from her.

Lola exhaled, tightening her hands in her lap as she looked out at the passing lights of the city, traveling east through Manhattan. He hadn't spoken once since she'd given him the address for her apartment in Murray Hill.

She pointed toward the nondescript apartment building. "That's it."

"Is there an attached garage?"

"Garage?" Her lips quirked. "There's not even a doorman."

With a sigh, he drove ahead until he found a parking spot on the street. Lola looked at the small parking space dubiously, but Rodrigo swerved the sports car into it with practiced ease. Opening her car door, he held out his hand.

Nervously, Lola took it. As he helped her out of the car, she tried not to notice how it felt to have his larger, stronger hand around her own.

He dropped her hand quickly and she shivered in her coat as they walked past trees with rattling brown leaves, in the heart of chilly November. She'd lived here for almost a year and liked it. It was a safe, comfortable neighborhood, not flashy but good for families, within walking distance of Grand Central Terminal. Her building was full of nice people, such as the kindly widow who occasionally watched Jett, as she was tonight.

Punching in her code to get in the door, she led him to the elevator, and then pressed the button for the fifth floor. At every moment, she was aware of him standing close beside her. They were alone, just the two of them, in this enclosed space.

She was relieved when they reached her floor. She hurried out of the elevator, then down the nondescript hallway.

Unlocking her door, she went inside. Rodrigo followed her closely, not touching, like a dark shadow.

Inside, her apartment was quiet, with only a single lamp on in the main room. The furniture had all come with the apartment and, though old, was comfortable enough.

A white-haired lady sat in an overstuffed chair next to the lamp. She looked up with a smile on her lips, knitting in her hands. "Lola, you're back early—"

The widow's eyes went wide when she saw Rodrigo, and no wonder. For the year Lola had lived here, she'd never invited any man to this apartment. Now, in the space of a single night, there'd been two different ones: Lola had left for the charity ball with Sergei and returned with Rodrigo.

When the kindly widow had told her she needed to get out and live a little, this probably wasn't what she'd had in mind.

"Hi, Mildred," Lola said. "Yes, I was feeling tired."

"Did you have a nice time?" the elderly woman said stiffly, looking at Rodrigo.

Lola never liked giving too much away. But she didn't want her neighbor to get the wrong idea. "This is Jett's father."

"Oh?" Her eyes went wide. She said with a big smile, *"Oh."*

"How was Jett tonight?" Lola said quickly, changing the subject.

"He was an angel. I gave him his bottle and bath. He's been asleep for about an hour." Gathering up her knitting, she rose to her feet, a grin on her wrinkled face as she looked between Lola and Rodrigo. "I'm sure you two have things to talk about."

Uh-oh. Now Mildred *was* getting the wrong idea. "There's no need to rush off—"

"Thank you for watching him," Rodrigo said gravely,

holding out a wad of hundred-dollar bills. The widow waved off the money.

"I'm happy to help. Jett's a little darling. I'm just glad you're finally here, after all this time," she added pointedly. "A baby needs a father. Just as a woman needs a husband."

With those firm words, the widow left.

"I definitely don't need a husband," Lola said, her cheeks burning.

"She thinks I abandoned you?" Rodrigo said, looking irritated.

She shrugged. "I've never spoken of you to anyone. Even my best friends don't know who Jett's father is." Her lips quirked at the corners. "I think they're under the impression that you're either married, abusive or a total alcoholic."

He glowered at her silently, his jaw tight.

Lola cleared her throat. "But you wanted to see Jett."

Hanging up her coat, she walked into the small apartment's only bedroom, motioning for him to follow.

A beam of moonlight pooled from the bedroom window to a spot between the bed and the crib wedged against the wall. Going to the crib, Lola looked down at her precious son. The four-month-old was sleeping peacefully, his chubby arms flung up over his head. A swell of love went through her.

"This is Jett," she whispered.

Rodrigo came up beside her, resting his powerful hands on the edge of the crib. He looked down at their sleeping baby. Lola's heart lifted to her throat as she looked between them.

Jett looked exactly like his father. She'd never realized it before, because she hadn't wanted to see it. But they had the same slight curl in their dark hair, the same black Spanish eyes. The baby yawned, showing a single dimple just like his father's. His dark lashes blinked sleepily.

The powerful media tycoon said in wonder, "He's so tiny."

"For now." A smile lifted her lips as she looked at him. "Someday he'll be as big as you."

For a long moment, they stood together, looking down at their son. She was aware of Rodrigo's hand just inches from hers. She could almost feel the warmth from his skin.

Suddenly, she yearned to tell him everything. To share things she'd never told even Hallie and Tess. Her friends thought Lola was so tough, but the truth was, she'd been scared, coming to New York alone after their breakup. She'd chosen it as her new home in a desperate, hopeless yearning to be closer to her little sisters, the only family she had left. Then she'd been too scared to contact them.

She'd thought of Rodrigo so many times during her pregnancy. When she'd gotten her first ultrasound. When she'd learned she was having a boy. When she'd gone into labor. And every day before, and since.

But she hadn't contacted him. Because she'd known the man she wanted—the man she'd loved—didn't exist. And in his place, with the same gorgeous, devastating body and heartbreaking dark eyes, was a man who could destroy her.

Now, Rodrigo lifted his gaze to hers. For a moment, she held her breath. Then his expression shuttered, his face turning cold.

"You should have told me."

"I couldn't," she whispered.

"I'm his father."

The baby stirred at Rodrigo's low, harsh voice. Alarmed, she put her finger to her lips and drew him out of the bedroom. Closing the bedroom door softly behind her, she whirled, glaring at him.

"You want to be a father? Then you should know the first rule of parenting is *Don't wake the baby*!"

He looked around the modest apartment. "I thought you said you got him a nice apartment."

"It's a wonderful place, you jerk!"

"You could have asked to stay at my loft in SoHo. I'm hardly ever there."

It was so pointlessly cruel, Lola sucked in her breath.

"You tossed me out of your house. You said I disgusted you and you never wanted to see me again! You think I would ever ask you for help after that? I'd die first!"

Her eyes were stinging. She blinked hard and fast. She wouldn't let herself cry. Only weak people, or children, cried in public and she hadn't been either for a long time.

Rodrigo's expression changed. He took a step toward her in the small apartment, his face half hidden by shadow.

"You don't need to ask for my help, or anyone else's, ever again." His voice was low. "Because if the paternity test proves he's my son, I'm going to marry you."

A rush went through her. A thrill of terror—or was it joy?

"What?" she whispered numbly.

"For his sake." His dark eyes burned through her. "You will be mine."

Lola's hazel eyes were astonished. As well they should be.

After three broken engagements, Rodrigo had never planned to propose again to anyone. For any reason. His youthful dreams of love and family and home were just that—dreams.

But looking at his sleeping son, he'd felt a hard shift in his soul that shocked him. Looking down at the baby's face, so much like his own, he'd remembered his own lonely childhood. And he'd vowed, to the depths of his soul, that his son would never feel like Rodrigo had once felt.

Jett would never believe his father didn't love him. He'd never feel like a burden, unwanted and unloved, as his parents left him in the care of nannies and neglected him for their own selfish romantic pursuits. His son would have a stable home. His parents would raise him together. There would be no instability in their family life, no revolving door of new lovers and spouses. They would be a family. With the same last name.

Lola might hate Rodrigo now, but she loved their son. That was clear in everything she'd done, even taking the million-dollar check that must have hurt her pride. But she'd done it, because she'd feared Rodrigo might try to take the baby from her.

She'd chosen custody of their son over the vast fortune Rodrigo could have offered her.

She'd made a mistake, taking the child from him. But he'd also made a mistake, believing the very worst of her.

For Jett's sake, he would try to forgive. They would start fresh. He would accept his responsibility to his son. Lola would do the same.

Or would she?

"Marry you?" She breathed, her eyes wide. "You're crazy."

"Our son deserves a stable home. Surely you can see that."

Lola's forehead furrowed. "He has one! With me!"

He said stiffly, "I'm willing to forgive you for stealing him from me—"

"I didn't steal him! I was protecting him!"

"But you have to realize that everything has changed now."

Her beautiful face looked numb. "It doesn't mean we have to marry. I know how you feel about marriage." She took a deep breath. "After all your fiancées cheated on you…"

Rodrigo stiffened, wondering how she'd heard. He certainly hadn't spoken about it over the years. But some people did know. His exes. Marnie. And gossip had a way of spreading, especially in his industry.

"This is different," he said coldly. "We're not in love."

She didn't look encouraged by this statement. Shaking her head, she lifted her chin stubbornly. "We can set up some kind of visitation schedule."

"Are you serious?" He raised his eyebrows. "Shuttling our baby from place to place, coast to coast? Always separated from one parent? Never really sure of where his home is? No."

"It doesn't have to be like that. Lots of healthy, happy children have parents who aren't married—"

"Not my son."

She glared at him. "Why marriage?"

Rodrigo couldn't explain to her what his childhood had been like. He'd never fully told anyone, not even the three women he'd claimed to love during his brief engagements long ago. He said shortly, "Is it so strange? I want us both to be there for our son. Every day. And for him to feel safe and loved."

"And you think he doesn't feel loved now?" she said indignantly.

"I know you love him, Lola. I can see it in everything you've done." She relaxed slightly, until he added, "Which is the reason you'll marry me."

She scowled. "I'm not marrying someone I don't love."

Rodrigo drew closer, looking down at her in the small apartment. "You used to love me. Once."

"I learned my lesson, didn't I?"

"Fine. You don't need to love me." His lips curled. "In fact, I'd prefer it if you don't. It keeps things simpler. But you will marry me, Lola. Soon." Straightening the cuffs of his tuxedo jacket, he said, "Sleep on it. Once you've calmed down, you'll see I'm right."

"I won't!"

Rodrigo looked down at her in the soft glow of the lamp-light. His voice was low. "This is a dangerous world. Much can happen. Accidents. Illness. People can die."

"Are you threatening me?" She gasped.

"What? No!" Jolted, he clawed his hand roughly through his dark hair. "I'm saying a child needs as much protection, as much security and love, as he can get. My parents died, Lola. One, then the other. What happened to yours?"

The blood drained from her face. She'd always refused to speak of her past, but now he knew his suspicions were right.

"You're an orphan," he guessed. Biting her lip, she looked away. "So our child already has a mark against him, with no grandparents to love him." He set his jaw. "I'm an only child. So no uncles or aunts."

Looking away, she muttered, "I have two sisters."

His eyebrows raised in surprise. "You do?"

Lola stared at the floor. "I haven't seen them for a long time."

Rodrigo sensed some pain there, but he didn't want to ask. He just pressed his advantage. "So already, our baby is more vulnerable, with no extended family. Don't you want him to have a father? Think of what I can give him. What I can give both of you."

She stiffened. "I don't need more money—"

"Not just money. My name. My time. My protection. My love."

She froze. "Your *love*."

"Yes. A father's love." He set his jaw. "Jett needs me as much as he needs you, Lola. I want to be there for him, to help raise him, to teach him how to be a man. Together, you and I can give him a better childhood than we had. Either of us."

He saw by her expression that his shot hit home. She

suddenly looked uncertain, her eyes luminous in the shadowy light.

Turning away, Rodrigo stopped at the door.

"My son will have my name, Lola. And so will you. This marriage will happen. Accept it." He gave her a hard smile. "Sleep well tonight. Because tomorrow, you're both coming home with me."

Rodrigo arrived the next day, as promised, bright and early. But his men came much sooner than that.

Lola peeked out the window again. Eight stories below, she still saw the black SUV parked across the street. It had arrived last night, thirty minutes after Rodrigo had left.

For all his fine words about marriage and family and love, she thought bitterly, he didn't trust her. He'd sent his henchmen to watch her apartment building to make sure she didn't try to flee with the baby.

They weren't even married yet, but he was already treating her like a prisoner.

But could she totally blame him? a small voice said inside her. She'd left California and kept their baby a secret for a year.

Shut up, she told that voice angrily.

But she'd finally come to the reluctant conclusion that Rodrigo was right. Their baby needed two parents, his whole family. Lola's own father had died when she was five, and she'd always felt that loss, somewhere in the back of her mind. In some ways, losing her father was the start of losing everything, because that was when her mom had had to go back to work. She'd earned only a fraction of what her father had, so they'd had to move out of their sunny three-bedroom house and into the trailer.

Now, Lola looked back at her small furnished apartment. She'd packed their meager possessions into three suitcases, leaving the dishware and odds and ends for the next tenant. She and Jett had been happy here, she thought wistfully.

Then she shook her head with a snort, remembering all the nights she'd cried herself to sleep over the last year. It was why she hadn't invited Hallie to stay here, when her friend had briefly needed a place to stay last summer. Lola couldn't bear to let anyone see her cry. Well, except Jett, but only because he'd cried even more.

Lola was supposed to be the strong one, the one her friends came to for advice and support, not the one who needed help. She'd pushed Hallie and Tess to get the financial support their babies deserved. She'd pushed them to get their lives together. And look at those two now—happy, in love, joyful. She'd helped them get there. *Speaking the brutal truth with love*, Lola called it, though her friends sometimes grumbled that her words could be more brutal than loving.

But they didn't know how scared Lola felt on the inside. She'd worked through her pregnancy because she was afraid to spend the money Rodrigo had thrown at her. Afraid that bad things could happen. And even after a year, she hadn't been brave enough to contact her baby sisters. Guilt still hung heavily over her at how she'd failed them at eighteen.

A child needs as much protection, as much security and love, as he can get. My parents died, Lola. One, then the other. What happened to yours?

She looked at Jett, now stretched out happily on a soft blanket over the rug. Rodrigo was right. As much as she hated to admit it. Jett deserved as much security and love as she could possibly give.

Because parents could die. They could get sick or go to jail. And even if Lola was ever brave enough to contact her sisters, they were still so young, Kelsey fifteen, Johanna only twelve. Whether they now hated her, or they'd forgotten her completely, the truth was, her sisters had a new family now. They'd been lost to her long ago.

Jett was all that mattered. She wanted him to be safe and loved. And from the moment Rodrigo had seen their baby, he'd seemed to feel the same.

Already our baby is more vulnerable, with no extended family. Don't you want him to have a father? Think of what I can give him... My name. My time. My protection. My love.

She'd barely slept that night, tossing and turning. Sometime around 3:00 a.m., she'd come to a decision.

She didn't love Rodrigo, and he didn't love her. But she would marry him. Their baby deserved that sacrifice.

Yet it wasn't easy. With a sinking heart, Lola looked back out the window and saw another car had arrived. She recognized, even at this distance, the gorgeous, arrogant man getting out of it. She swallowed hard. Then her jaw set.

Fine, they would marry. But it would be on her terms.

She heard the intercom buzz, and his husky voice demanding entrance. She pressed the button to let him in downstairs. Putting on her coat, Lola picked up her baby. Tucking his blanket into her diaper bag, she waited with a sense of dread.

A few minutes later, she heard heavy steps in the hallway. A hard knock sounded at her door. With a deep breath, she opened it.

Rodrigo's dark eyes burned through her. "You are ready?"

So much was encompassed in that simple question.

"Yes," she said.

"Good." Relaxing slightly, he strode into the apartment, looking so handsome she almost couldn't bear it. He wore a long, open black cashmere coat that revealed the shape of his broad shoulders and biceps, with a well-cut black shirt and trousers beneath. He was followed inside by his driver and bodyguard, both of whom she knew slightly from the old days.

"Have a long night, did you, boys?" she said to them dryly. As they gathered the suitcases, they glanced at each other. Rodrigo's smile widened.

"You knew they were watching?"

"Of course I knew," she snapped at him. "You're not very trusting."

"I'm glad you didn't try to run."

She pressed her lips together. "There was no point. You convinced me that you're right."

"I'm always right." But even as he spoke the arrogant words, his dark eyes looked her over appreciatively. As befitted the cold November weather, she wore a form-fitting black puffy coat, with a faux-fur-edged hood, and a hem that stretched down over her hips. Her legs were covered with black leggings and her black boots matched her hood, edged with faux fur.

Against her will, she blushed beneath his glance. It enraged her. Why did he still have that effect on her? It didn't seem fair!

"Is this all, Miss Price?" asked the bodyguard.

"And the stroller by the door."

As his two henchmen left the apartment with the suitcases and stroller, Rodrigo held out his arm. "Come."

"Wait."

At the breathless sound of her voice, Rodrigo looked down at her questioningly.

"Like I said. I realized you're right. Jett needs a stable home, and a father to raise him. We should marry. Even though we don't love each other." Her voice trembled a little. "It's best for Jett." She paused. "But—"

"But?" His voice was low and dangerous.

She lifted her gaze. "I just want to make sure we understand each other. This marriage is for duty. For convenience."

"Convenience?" he repeated.

How could he not know what she meant?

"In…in name only," she whispered, her teeth suddenly chattering.

He gave a low, hard laugh, his dark eyes glittering in the morning light. "Is that what you think?"

"I mean it, Rodrigo—"

"No." He cupped her cheek. "You don't."

His eyes burned through her, and he slowly lowered his head toward hers.

She sucked in her breath as, against her will, a fire of desire swept through her body that she was helpless to deny. Her toes curled in anticipation, and she closed her eyes, holding her breath, waiting for him to kiss her.

At the last moment before his lips would have touched hers, he stopped. Confused, she opened her eyes.

His face was cruel as he looked down at her with a cold, mocking smile. "In name only, *querida*?"

Her cheeks suddenly burned. "You arrogant bastard—"

"Come. We have a busy day planned."

His eyes softened as they rested on the dark-haired baby against her hip. He caressed the baby tenderly on the head. "We will be a family soon, *pequeño*." Then he gave Lola a smile that didn't meet his eyes. "No more talk of *convenient* marriages. You will be conveniently in my bed. And soon."

"In your dreams," she retorted. For answer, he gave her a sensual smile.

"Yes. I have dreamed of it, Lola," he said huskily. "And soon those dreams will be reality."

Her eyes widened at his admission, and her mouth snapped shut as she recalled all the hot nights when she, too, had dreamed of him. Fuming, she followed him out of the apartment.

When they reached the street, she saw one of his men placing the suitcases in the back of the black SUV, as the other put the stroller in the back of Rodrigo's sleek luxury sedan.

Lola frowned. "Where are we going?"

Rodrigo opened the sedan door. "A few places."

Seeing a brand-new baby seat latched securely into the sedan's back seat, she wondered if his longtime executive assistant, Marnie, had arranged it. She'd always hated that smug busybody, now more than ever. "Where?"

"You'll see."

As the SUV turned south, Rodrigo drove Lola and the baby north, to a cutting-edge private clinic on the Upper East Side. As far as she could tell, it had opened up on Sunday, bringing in a full staff, just for their paternity test. Within two hours, they had the results. Jett was Rodrigo's son.

"I knew it," Rodrigo said quietly when he got the results.

Lola looked at him irritably. "Then why did you insist on a test?"

"There's knowing, and there's knowing."

"That makes no sense. You could have just trusted me."

"I needed proof." He didn't explain further. When it came to asking for help or showing weakness, Rodrigo was even worse than Lola.

After the clinic, the next stop that morning turned out to be the prestigious white-shoe Manhattan law firm of Crosby, Flores and Jackson, where, amid the hushed elegance of a private office, Lola was presented with a fifty-page legal contract of a prenuptial agreement.

Sitting at the gleaming mahogany desk, she read through it slowly, to the obvious surprise of the lawyers, marking up any clause she didn't like with a red pen.

Lola had made below average grades in school, but she'd always been good at debate. It was why, when she was twelve, her mother had handed Lola the phone if she needed to convince the electric company to turn the lights back on, or deal with a debt collector. It was also how, after Lola's failed attempt at a "quick and easy" movie star career, she'd eventually become executive assistant to a powerful tycoon. Lola knew how to absorb and how to deflect. She knew when to pay attention and how.

In short, she knew how to argue.

Even opaque legal language couldn't confuse her. It was like following a shell game. You just never took your eyes off the ball.

Finally, she set down the papers.

"I have some changes," she said coolly.

"Do you?" Rodrigo's voice was amused.

"Yes. Starting with this clause in paragraph Four C…"

In the end, Lola got what she wanted. She negotiated away one financial item after another—the amount of money set aside for alimony, child support, housing and staff levels in case of a divorce—in order to keep the one thing she actually cared about, which was primary custody of Jett. That was the one thing she was never, ever willing to lose.

She marveled that Rodrigo seemed focused on something else entirely: making sure Lola would be punished if she were ever unfaithful during their marriage.

She was amazed he'd be worried about that. As she'd told him, she'd never kissed another man in her whole life. But as she'd heard from a gossipy production assistant, he'd had three fiancées cheat on him. So maybe she could understand, after all.

Whatever the reason, Lola gladly used it to her advantage. The prenuptial agreement was altered. In case of divorce, no matter which of them was at fault, Lola would get custody of Jett. But if she ever cheated on Rodrigo, even after thirty years of marriage, she wouldn't get a penny. No alimony. No marital property. Nothing but the three suitcases she'd arrived with.

But since she obviously wouldn't cheat, she'd won. She smiled as they left the law office.

"You never thought of becoming a lawyer?" Rodrigo murmured, his dark eyes gleaming as they pushed the baby's stroller out of the wood-paneled private office.

"Lawyer?" Lola snorted. "Me?"

"You think like one."

She shook her head. "I'm not even sure if I passed my GED test."

They left the law office and got back into the car. As Rodrigo drove her and the baby south toward his SoHo loft, he suddenly asked, "Why did you drop out of high school?"

She looked at him guardedly. "What do you mean?"

"You're smart, Lola. A fighter." He shook his head wryly. "Something I've sometimes learned the hard way. Why didn't you go to college? Why did you drop out of high school and go to LA and do—" he hesitated "—what you did?"

Her cheeks suddenly burned. "I had my reasons."

She couldn't explain why, at eighteen, she'd been so desperate to earn money, so stupid and naive, that she'd done things she wasn't proud of. Things that had caused Rodrigo to call her ugly names, six years later. She hadn't done everything Marnie had accused her of—not even close—but what she'd done was bad enough. And she'd still failed to save her sisters.

But she wasn't going to explain and let Rodrigo think she was a weakling and a failure, in addition to being a— well, he'd never actually called her a whore. But that was how he'd made her feel.

Wrapping her arms around herself, she looked stonily

out the window. Silence fell in the luxury sedan as he drove south through Manhattan, the only sound the yawns of their baby in his car seat behind them.

"You've always been quick," he said, his hands tightening on the steering wheel. "If you'd stayed in school—"

"I don't want to talk about it."

"You could have gone far. You could be a big-time lawyer or CEO of a major corporation by now. Why didn't anyone convince you to even try?"

She didn't look at him. A lump lifted to her throat.

She had been good in school once. When she was seven, she'd loved to puzzle over math and read. But after her father's death, her mother had been too busy and exhausted to help with school. Later, she'd remarried. After Lola's two half-siblings were born—and especially after her new stepfather was injured on the job—school had become a luxury. It just wasn't important anymore, not like making sure there was food in the fridge, and caring for her sisters when her stepfather was passed out drunk, and their mother working the overnight shift.

When Lola was fifteen, her mother had died. Bonnie had been feeling bad for months, but put off seeing the doctor, insisting she didn't have money or time. By the time she'd finally gotten her diagnosis, the cancer was terminal. She'd lived only a few months after that. Her stepfather, trying to cope with the grief and his family's sudden lack of income, ended up going to prison for dealing drugs. There had been nothing left to hold their family together.

Staring hard out the window of the luxury sedan, Lola wiped her eyes fiercely. She hadn't even told Hallie and Tess that. Just as she'd never told them anything about her baby's father, not even Rodrigo Cabrera's name.

It was the only way Lola knew how to deal with that kind of radioactive pain. To pretend it didn't exist.

"I didn't care, all right?" she said numbly, staring hard out the window. "I never cared about college."

"What do you care about, then?"

Lola thought of her family. Everyone she'd lost. Everyone she'd loved but been unable to save.

Setting her jaw, she whispered, "Protecting what's mine."

CHAPTER THREE

The early November morning was cold and gray as Rodrigo turned the car down Prince Street, turning on Mercer.

Lola rolled down the window, breathing the cool air, relishing the feel against her hot skin. The air made her shiver. Or maybe it was the thought that she'd soon be Rodrigo's wife. She looked up at the lowering sky. She wondered what Hallie and Tess would say when they were invited to Lola's wedding out of the blue.

Her lips quirked. They would be surprised, to say the least.

She'd met Hallie Hatfield and Tess Foster last year at a New York single moms' support group. They'd been the only ones who were pregnant, and they'd soon realized that none of them had told the fathers about the babies.

Her friends were both now happily married. While Lola just prayed she wasn't making a horrible mistake.

Rodrigo pulled his sedan to the front of a fashionable prewar building in SoHo, where a doorman took his keys.

"Good morning, Mr. Cabrera. In the garage like always?"

"Thank you, Andrews," Rodrigo said, walking around the car to get the stroller from the trunk. The doorman's eyes widened when he saw it, and even more when he saw Lola get out and take their baby in her arms.

Tucking sleepy Jett into the stroller, Lola followed Rodrigo into the lobby of the luxurious building, and into an elevator that he accessed with a fingerprint.

On the top floor, the elevator opened directly onto a private foyer. And Lola entered the penthouse loft she hadn't visited in over a year.

Shivering, she looked around the large, bohemian penthouse loft. Colorful furniture filled the enormous space, and huge windows showed an expansive, unrestricted southern view of the city, to the skyscrapers of Lower Manhattan. She could dimly see the steel and glass building where she'd once worked for Sergei Morozov. Strange to think that Rodrigo could have been unknowingly looking at her, whenever he'd visited New York. So close, but so far apart.

The bare brick walls were decorated with old original movie posters, along with old neon signs, which were no doubt originals, too. Rodrigo had occasionally seen neon signs he liked as he traveled to his movie sets around the world, from Tokyo to Sydney to Berlin. She'd watched in awe as he'd casually bought entire businesses, simply to acquire the signs.

That was Rodrigo, Lola thought, a little bitterly. He'd rip out someone's beating heart just to tap his toe to the rhythm.

She blinked hard, to make sure no trace of emotion was on her face. She might become his wife, but he'd never possess her. She'd never let herself love him, ever again.

"Miss Price!" The New York housekeeper, Mrs. Farrow, came in from the next room of the loft. The woman's plump face broke into a big smile. "I'm so glad you're back. And how exciting, you're going to be married?"

"Strange, huh?" Lola said, feeling awkward. Especially when the woman was followed by a white-haired, distinguished-looking man Lola didn't know.

"Not strange. Lovely." Mrs. Farrow knelt before the stroller, smiling at Jett. "And this is your baby?"

"Yes… Jett."

The older woman beamed. "He's adorable."

Pulling off her black gloves, one by one, Lola stuck them in her pockets. "Thank you."

The white-haired man smiled at her, his eyes twinkling beneath bushy white brows. "So should we get this show on the road?"

Lola frowned at Rodrigo. "What's he talking about?"

"This is the judge," he said. "He's going to marry us."

"What? When?"

"Today." Rodrigo's lips curved. "Now."

Lola stared at him in shock.

"We can't," she stammered. "We need a marriage license."

"Occasionally, when there's a good reason, the rules can be bent."

"What's the good reason?"

His black eyes gleamed. "It's Sunday. And I wish to marry you today. Not wait to get the license from City Hall tomorrow and then wait another twenty-four hours after that." He turned to the judge. "Shall we begin, your honor?"

"Now?" Lola's head was spinning. "No! I want a real ceremony! With my friends!"

Rodrigo's sensual lips curved sardonically. "Sorry to crush all your romantic dreams," he said, as if he was sure she didn't actually have any. "You'll have to settle—" he reached into his pocket "—for this."

Holding up a small black velvet box, he opened it to reveal an engagement ring. Her eyes went wide. The diamond was as huge as a robin's egg.

"We have everything else we need. Witnesses." He looked at Mrs. Farrow, and Tobias, the bodyguard who'd just come in through the front door. "A judge." Tilting his head, he said courteously to the white-haired man, "I hope your daughter is doing well."

"Yes, and I'll never forget how you helped her," the judge said warmly. "My four grandchildren still have a mother today thanks to you."

Rodrigo acknowledged his praise with a slight nod. "I was glad to pay for the experimental treatment. I'm pleased it worked. And grateful for your help."

"What, marrying you two?" The judge's voice was genial. "Marrying folks is my favorite part of the job! I'll make sure the paperwork's all handled right." Then, looking at Lola, he faltered. "Of course, only if the lady is willing."

"I'm not," she said flatly.

"Excuse us for a moment." Grabbing her arm, Rodrigo pulled her back to the foyer. "What do you think you're doing?"

Lifting her snoozing, limp baby from the stroller, she glared at him fiercely. "I'm not getting married without my friends!"

"Which friends are you hoping to see?" Rodrigo's voice was dangerous and low. "A certain lovelorn Russian, to try to make me jealous?"

Lola looked at him in shock, then burst into a laugh. "Sergei? You can't be serious!"

"I don't intend to wait." His expression hardened. "We're getting married. Right now."

"Or else what?"

"Do not defy me."

"Is that a threat?"

His voice changed. "Marrying me today will benefit you as well."

"How?"

"It goes both ways. Perhaps if we wait—" he tilted his head thoughtfully "—I'll get cold feet and decide to call it all off."

"Fine with me—"

"Perhaps I'll decide I'd rather sue for full custody, and

take my chances in the courts. I can wait out a long trial. Can you?"

She glared at him.

He smiled.

Lola looked down at her baby's fuzzy jacket, breathing in his sweet baby scent. "I don't appreciate ham-fisted threats."

He shrugged. "I despise long engagements—"

"Long!"

"I want to get this done." His gaze hardened. "Is there any reason to delay?"

Her friends, she thought desperately. She wanted Tess and Hallie here for emotional support. And what about her little sisters? She hadn't seen them for seven years, but it felt wrong not to have her only family here.

But she couldn't be vulnerable enough to show weakness. Especially not with Rodrigo.

Instead, she indicated her black puffy jacket and leggings. "Does this look like a wedding dress to you?"

Taking off his cashmere coat, he glanced down at his own black shirt and trousers and gave a sardonic smile. "We are both wearing black, which seems appropriate for the occasion."

"Meaning what? This is like a funeral for you?" Hurt rushed through her, followed by anger. "If you're having second thoughts about marriage…"

His dark eyes turned hard. "I'm not. And neither are you." He looked down at her. "It happens now."

Her heart sank. So there would be no pleasant pre-wedding afternoon at the day spa with Tess and Hallie. No deep intense conversations over champagne as they helped her get ready to be a bride. They wouldn't be here to support her as she pledged her life to the man who'd broken her heart. The man who'd judged her past mistakes and made it clear he didn't think she was good enough. The man who'd tossed her love back in her face, and would never, ever, have wanted to marry her if not for Jett.

Lola would face it alone. Dressed for a funeral.

She took a deep breath.

"Fine," she said coldly. "Let's get it over with."

They returned to the main room of the loft.

"We're ready," Rodrigo told the judge.

"There's no rush, you know." The white-haired man suddenly looked nervous, glancing between them as if wondering what he'd gotten himself into, and how he could get himself out of it. "Marriage is, after all, a solemn occasion. Now that I think about it, there's a reason why the State of New York, in its infinite wisdom, instituted a twenty-four-hour waiting period—"

"Just do it," Rodrigo said harshly. His hand gripped her shoulder.

"Please," whispered Lola, ignoring the lump in her throat.

The judge hesitated. Then the baby gave a sudden sleepy whimper in Lola's arms, and she and Rodrigo both turned to comfort him. Watching them caring together for their son, tucking the baby back into the stroller for his nap, the judge seemed reassured. He gave a decisive nod when they returned.

"Very well. Ladies and gentlemen," he intoned. "We are gathered here today, in the presence of witnesses, to unite this man and this woman in the bonds of matrimony…"

The short ceremony passed quickly. As if in a dream, Lola heard herself speak the words that bound her to Rodrigo for life.

But the awful truth was, she'd bound herself to him long ago, from the night she'd become pregnant with his child.

And now, from this moment on, forever.

Rodrigo's dark eyes gleamed down at her as the ceremony drew to a close. He seemed almost surprised. Why?

Had he thought for some reason that something would prevent it?

Their eyes locked as he slid that obscenely huge diamond on her finger. Funny. Once, she would have dreamed of a moment like this. At fourteen, she dreamed of love, and a handsome prince. At eighteen, she would have just been keen to hock the ring.

And now, at twenty-five, how different this moment felt from anything she'd imagined!

"…I now pronounce you husband and wife." The judge looked between them with a wink. "You may now kiss the bride."

Kiss?

Lola looked up at the man who was now her husband. *I feel nothing*, she told herself desperately. *Nothing.*

As Rodrigo lowered his head toward hers, she put her hand up to stop him. His chest felt so powerful, so muscular, that in spite of herself, she shivered. "What about your wedding band?" His left hand was still bare. "Don't you need a ring, too?"

"I'm a man. I don't need jewelry to feel married."

She stiffened at his sexist remark. But before she could protest, he took her roughly into his arms.

"Mrs. Cabrera," he whispered.

Her lips parted in shock as she heard him speak her new name. Ruthlessly, he lowered his mouth to hers.

His lips were hot and sweet, tasting of spice and fire. As he kissed her, the world started to spin. Feeling the strength and power of his body against her own, she gripped his shoulders for balance. She forgot everything in her own aching need. She'd wanted him for so long. A sigh rose from deep inside her, the recognition that this man was hers, hers alone, as she had always been his…

The judge, housekeeper and bodyguard watching them

applauded, and Lola suddenly remembered they had an audience.

Pulling away, Rodrigo looked down at her with gleaming eyes.

Pleasure was still spiraling through her as her lips tingled from his bruising kiss. When his mouth had claimed hers, all the distance between them, all the coldness and anger, had exploded into fire, like two storms colliding. But now the distance was back.

She tried to read his expression, to see if the kiss had affected him like it had her. But his face gave nothing away. "Thank you," he said to the judge, then turned to the bodyguard, Tobias. "Everything is ready for our departure?"

"Already packed, Mr. Cabrera."

"Packed?" Lola frowned at her brand-new husband. "Are you going somewhere?"

"Not me. *We*." Rodrigo gave her a smile that didn't meet his eyes. "My jet is waiting to take us to Los Angeles."

It was like a splash of ice water, jolting her awake. "But New York is my home now. My sisters—all my friends—"

His lips twisted. "Friends like Morozov?"

"He was never my friend!"

He snorted. "Exactly."

Lola ground her teeth. "Why are you being so unreasonable!"

"You just agreed to be my wife, Lola. To honor and obey." Rodrigo gave her a cruel smile. Cupping her cheek, he looked down at her as he said softly, "Now you will."

Rodrigo could hardly believe it.

After all his engagements that had never made it to the altar, this one actually had. They were married. He was almost in shock.

Perhaps it was true he'd rushed their vows that morning. But once he'd made up his mind to marry her, he couldn't give Lola a chance to betray him like the rest. He couldn't take any chances with fate, or whatever else had cursed his life.

This marriage would work. It had to work. They had a child.

Now, as Rodrigo drove his red convertible north, traveling from the private airport outside Los Angeles to his beach house near Malibu, Rodrigo glanced at the rearview mirror. He saw his baby's pudgy hand waving from the rear-facing baby seat. Jett was making cooing noises, and seemed delighted to be in California, beneath the palm trees and warm blue skies.

It was strange to think he had a child. Even stranger for Rodrigo to think he was a father. What did he know about fatherhood?

His own parents had left him in the care of nannies. His mother, an American actress, had traveled the world enjoying her love affairs, as the man who'd supposedly been his father, Francisco Cabrera, had tortured himself with jealousy pursuing the unfaithful wife he adored.

It wasn't until Francisco's funeral, when Rodrigo was twenty-one, that his mother told him the reason the man always seemed to despise him. Rodrigo's real father had been the chauffeur.

"He was very handsome, and I was bored, what can I say?" Elizabeth Cabrera had told him, putting her finger to her cheek thoughtfully. "It was just a one-night indiscretion. Francisco wanted me to get rid of you. Perhaps I should have. My figure was never quite the same after."

Now, Rodrigo glanced in the rearview mirror of the convertible, toward his son. Jett was such a sweet little boy, with big black eyes and chubby cheeks. He'd been obviously well fed and well cared for. Obviously loved. Beneath Lola's ferocity, there was utter devotion for their son.

He appreciated that about her, at least.

In some ways, their new relationship was simple: they were a family. But between Rodrigo and Lola, now husband and wife, it was a little more complicated.

His gaze now shifted to his wife, sitting beside him in the convertible. Her arms were folded, and she was seething silently at the wide Pacific Ocean as they drove up the coastal highway. He smiled grimly.

He hadn't lied when he'd said she was smart and a fighter. She'd been the best personal assistant he'd ever had, even better than Marnie, his longest-serving secretary. He'd relied on Lola's intelligence, on her strength. She'd been a miracle worker as an employee, always able to achieve the impossible, willing to work any hour of the day or night, even on Christmas Day.

For two years, he'd wanted her. But he hadn't let himself even flirt. Then, after Lola had kissed him in Mexico City, he'd taken her to bed, and discovered she was a virgin. From that moment, they'd been intoxicated, drunk on passion and pleasure. When she'd told him she loved him, in spite of everything, his heart had expanded in his chest.

Then Marnie had given him those awful photographs of Lola half-naked in that chair, looking seductively into the camera. And there was more.

Sir, there's something you should know about Lola Price.
Rodrigo still felt sick thinking about it.

But why had Lola ever done those sordid things at eighteen? The thought jolted him. Because she clearly wasn't the coldhearted gold digger he'd once believed her to be. If she'd cared only about money, she would have demanded a huge payout from Rodrigo the moment she'd discovered she was pregnant.

So why had Lola posed for those provocative photographs? Why had she done even worse? Just youthful stupidity? He ground his teeth. He'd had his share of that himself, with his own three broken engagements. But was there more to it? Had she just been desperate to be a movie star? Or had something forced her into it?

Rodrigo looked at Lola out of the corner of his eye. The warm wind was tossing her blond hair in the sun. But her jaw was tight, and she was tapping her fingertips on the convertible's armrest in repressed fury.

No point in asking her, he knew. She guarded the darkest secrets of her soul with grim determination. In that, she and Rodrigo were the same.

During the flight from New York on his private jet, they'd sat at opposite ends of the cabin, ignoring each other. She'd accused him of bossing her around, being a tyrant. Not a great start. But it wouldn't go on for long.

His gaze traced down the curve of her cheek, to her swanlike throat and full breasts. He'd promised to honor and cherish her, forsaking all others. She didn't realize that he'd already done that for the last year. He was hungry for her. Starving.

He wanted her in his bed. Tonight.

But first, he needed her to actually look at him. He grudgingly extended an olive branch.

"Are you really so upset about leaving New York?"

"You had no right," Lola said, turning to him with her eyes blazing. "Just because I'm your wife doesn't mean I'm your slave. I wanted to stay in New York, but you didn't care! Just like you didn't care you frog-marched me through our wedding!"

"You wanted Morozov there?"

She let loose a curse that would have made a sailor blush.

"Not Morozov, then," he said, amused. "Then who?"

"My friends. Hallie. Tess." She looked disconsolately out at the hills. "My sisters."

"You said you haven't seen your sisters in years."

"I haven't," she whispered.

"Then I don't see why it matters that they weren't there today."

Lola took a deep breath. "They're a lot younger than me. Still just kids. My mother died when they were just five and eight. They were sent to foster care, then adopted." Her jaw tightened. "When I left California last year, I went to New York. I intended to finally ask them to forgive me. For not keeping my promise to get custody back." She looked down at her hands, twisting in her lap. "But I never had the guts."

Admitting failure was so unlike Lola that he glanced at her in surprise. He switched gears, stepping hard on the gas as they drove up the highway. "You'll think of some way to smooth things over. You always do."

Lola looked at him hopefully out of the corner of her eye. "You think so?"

He snorted. "You never had trouble arranging people when you were my assistant. You always managed to get me appointments with anyone from feared dictators to beloved religious leaders."

"Because you're you."

"And you're you," he said firmly. "You know how to argue people into things. When you're ready to see your sisters, you'll figure out how."

Lola bit her lip thoughtfully. He could almost see the wheels start to turn in her mind. "I could send them some amazing present. Just to break the ice. Then they'd have to contact me to say thanks."

"That could work," he said, smiling. He was glad to see some of the dark cloud lift from her shoulders—and glad to distract her from being angry at him for rushing her into marriage and back to California.

"It could." She smiled back, and it was warmer and brighter than the California sun.

Then her lips twisted mischievously. "I'm warning you. The gift will probably be expensive."

Rodrigo shrugged. "Spend whatever you like. What's mine is yours."

"Do you mean that?"

"I already know you didn't marry me for my money, Lola."

"No." Her expression darkened. She turned away, her arm resting on the edge of the convertible as she looked out at the ocean. "I married you because you blackmailed me."

The brief moment of camaraderie, of shared sunshine, abruptly disappeared.

Rodrigo turned the convertible off the highway, traveling down a private lane to the edge of tall stone walls that blocked off his compound. He punched in the security code, and the gate slid open. He drove the convertible inside the courtyard, followed closely by his longtime bodyguard, Tobias Watson, in the SUV with all the luggage.

"Back to home sweet home," he murmured.

"Yes," Lola said, looking up at the beach house.

Getting out of the convertible, he reached in the back seat of the convertible to unbuckle their baby.

"I can do that," she said, alarmed.

"It's done." Gently, he lifted their baby from the car seat and held him in his arms. Lola looked panicked, and then, looking closer, confused.

"You're holding him correctly," she said, clearly shocked. She looked at his face. "How did you learn to hold a baby?"

"You think I'm completely incompetent?" Rodrigo drawled.

"You've never held a baby in your life."

"Then I must be a natural." He didn't bother to explain that while she'd been studiously ignoring him on the flight, when he'd been working on his laptop, he'd actually been reading articles about the proper care and handling of infants. He wasn't going to let Lola lord her greater knowledge over him, or be forced to ask her for the favor of teaching him what to do.

Once, he would have asked her, without thought, and been willing to humble himself for her. But not anymore. Their relationship was still on too shaky a footing for that. It probably hadn't helped that he'd bullied her into marriage and returning to California. But he had no regrets. It was the most efficient means of getting what he wanted.

As they walked toward his sprawling, luxurious beach house, the front door opened. His executive assistant, Marnie McAdam, appeared in the doorway, her eyes eager behind her thick glasses. "You're back—" Her expression changed when she saw Lola and the baby. "What...what's she doing here?"

For an answer, Lola lifted her left hand in a movement so violent it was almost an obscene gesture, to show her the huge diamond ring.

Marnie's eyes went wide as she looked between them. "You're married?"

"Isn't it wonderful news?" Lola said.

His assistant looked pale. A year older than Rodrigo, Marnie McAdam had been a college graduate traveling in Madrid when he'd hired her as his first employee at his new company, Cabrera Media Group, after he'd taken over his father's small studio. Over the last fifteen years, Rodrigo had come to depend on Marnie for her dedication and loyalty. Before Lola had arrived, she'd been his top assistant.

No wonder the two women hadn't liked each other. Marnie was the one who'd told Rodrigo about Lola's past, telling him all the awful facts as she'd put the photographs in his hands.

And Lola knew it. She gave the older woman a hard smile.

He had the sudden alarming image of the two women

coming to blows. He was fairly sure Lola, with her hard-edged fearlessness, would emerge the victor. He had no desire to see Marnie in the hospital, so he stepped abruptly between them.

"That'll be all for today, Marnie. You can head home."

"Whose baby?" She breathed unsteadily, looking at Jett in his arms.

"Mine," he said.

"You didn't know?" said Lola sweetly. "I thought you might have arranged things for us in New York."

"No," Rodrigo said. "She didn't." He looked at Marnie. "We might need some additional baby furniture, though. I'll contact you later."

"Of course, Mr. Cabrera." Turning to Lola, she said, "Congratulations."

Lola glared at her. "You heard what he said. Get going."

Biting her lip, Marnie looked at Rodrigo.

"Thank you, Marnie," he said, more kindly.

With a nod, she turned and hurried to her car. As the older woman drove out of the gate, Rodrigo turned on Lola coldly. "Was that really necessary?"

His wife didn't answer. Taking the yawning baby from his arms, she strode ahead of him into the beach house, proud and scornful as a queen.

Irritated, he followed her into the house's enormous great room, with its wall of windows overlooking the beach and bright blue ocean.

"You can't hate Marnie for telling me the truth about your past."

"The truth?" Lola looked at him incredulously. "Is that what you think?"

"Are you saying you didn't pose for those pictures? You didn't let that man—" But he couldn't go on. Just remembering the rest of Marnie's report still made his blood boil with unwilling jealousy and rage.

Lola's lovely face was pale as she turned away. "I need to put Jett to bed."

"Wait. I'm talking to you—"

"Not now." Behind them, two bodyguards were bringing in suitcases from the SUV. Lola pointed at her suitcases. "Can you please take those to the baby's room?"

"Baby's room?" Tobias Watson asked, frowning.

Glancing at Rodrigo, she said coolly, "I assume there is one."

"I told Mrs. Lee to arrange the best guest room," he said grudgingly.

As the bodyguard nodded and started down the hall, Lola said without looking at Rodrigo, "I'll be sleeping in there, too."

Without another word, she collected the diaper bag and swept down the hallway, leaving Rodrigo alone in the great room with the amazing view of the Pacific.

He ground his teeth.

But he could understand why Lola was already so defensive and irritable. Part of him felt the same. Having her back here, in this house where they'd once been lovers, gave him a sense of vertigo, like an earthquake beneath his feet. Wistful memories of their love affair still lingered in every room.

Looking slowly around, Rodrigo gave an involuntary shiver. *There* he'd made love to her against the wall. *There* they'd lazed Sunday mornings on the sofa. He looked out through the double-story windows. Closing his eyes, he felt the sun burning hot and bright against his face, without the gentle mercy of clouds.

And *there*, on that white sand beach, one moonlit night beside the bonfire as the Santa Ana winds blew, Lola had told him she loved him. For answer, Rodrigo had taken her in his arms and kissed her hungrily, as she'd clung to him as if her life depended on it. The explosive heat of that sensual night! He shivered at the memory. They'd always been scrupulously careful about protection, but that one time, they'd been carried away by passion. Which was another way of saying they lost their minds. It was almost certainly the night she'd conceived their baby.

Turning away, he went to the wet bar and poured himself a drink. A few minutes later, when Lola returned from the baby's nursery, he saw her before she saw him. She'd long since taken off her coat, but she still wore the same black shirt, leggings and boots she'd been married in. He suddenly yearned to take those off, too. To feel the warmth of her naked skin.

A flash of heat went through him.

He gulped the last of his Scotch, letting it burn his throat as he set down the glass with a bang. "You're not sleeping in the nursery, Lola. I thought I made myself clear. You're sleeping in the bedroom. With me."

She whirled to face him, her beautiful face wild. "Forget it."

Rodrigo took an unwilling step toward her.

"I can't," he whispered. "I can't forget."

The memory of all the times he'd kissed her in this house, all the nights he'd made love to her, all their moments of laughter and lazy sensuality and joy burned through him. He had to clench his hands at his sides to keep himself from pulling her roughly into his arms.

"You forgot me long ago." Lola looked at him in the warm pink and gold light of the late afternoon sun, her eyes bright. "I'm sure you've had lovers here by the score since you tossed me out."

"Wrong," he said.

He heard her intake of breath. "What?"

Coming forward, Rodrigo cupped her cheek.

"I've had no other woman here. None," he whispered. Slowly, he ran his thumb along her tender bottom lip. "Not here, nor anywhere else. For the last year, I've hungered for you, Lola. Only for you."

"I…" She breathed, trembling beneath his touch. "I can't believe it…"

"All this time, I've wanted you." Pulling her body against his own, he whispered, "And now you're mine, I'm never going to let you go…"

His lips lowered to hers in a hard, passionate kiss. He held her body fast against his own, giving her no chance to resist. But she didn't even try. With a soft sigh, she reached her arms up to twist around his shoulders, pulling him down against her with the same hunger.

And in that moment, the kiss that had started as a mark of possession began to explode in pure light.

Lola hadn't realized it would be so hard to be back in this California beach house. The short months of their affair had been the happiest of her life.

Until her past had caught up with her. The most humiliating mistakes of her life. And when he'd discovered them, he'd tossed her aside as if she meant nothing.

Because she hadn't. Rodrigo had never loved her. Not even a little.

But Lola had still been stupid enough to love him.

Returning to this house today, she'd felt memories burn through her like acid. As she'd tucked their baby into the crib of his lavish new nursery, Lola looked at the little sofa nearby and vowed to herself that she'd sleep there alone every night. But she hadn't quite believed it, even then. Not when her traitorous body was yearning to be back in Rodrigo's bed.

Now, as her husband kissed her, his lips seemed pure fire.

His powerful arms tightened around her in the sunlit great room of the beach house, with the wide view of the white sand and blue Pacific. His mouth was hot and rough against hers. And the thought of any path that didn't end with them falling into bed was impossible.

So what? she thought suddenly. Sex didn't have to mean anything. It didn't mean love. It could be just a benefit of marriage, like filing jointly for taxes.

Lola closed her eyes in ecstasy as he pressed her against the wall, kissing slowly down her throat. She felt the heat of his lips against her skin. His hands gripped her wrists, as if to prevent her from running away.

As if she could, when this was all she wanted.

Her eyes fluttered open as he picked her up in his arms, as if she weighed nothing at all. His footsteps echoed against the red tile floors, his dark gaze unreadable as he carried her down the hallway to the enormous master bedroom.

White stucco walls surrounded the enormous bed, with its four large posters of black twisting wood, and a magnificent view.

Held in his arms, Lola looked back up at his face. The last time he'd brought her here, it had all been joy and laughter and passion. Because she'd loved him, even if he hadn't loved her back.

Now, everything they'd once had was lost.

Or was it?

No other woman. She still couldn't believe it. Even hating her, he had been faithful to her? That didn't make sense. Why would he be faithful?

The hazy golden light of late afternoon poured in from the west-facing windows as he set her on the bed, in a pool of warm sunlight. His eyes were dark as he stood above her, beside the bed. Never taking his eyes off her, he loosened the cuffs of his black shirt, then the buttons.

Her heart was in her throat as she looked up at him. The golden light caressed the hard planes and curves of his powerful, muscular chest, laced with dark hair. He was even more hard-bodied than the last time they'd been lovers, making her wonder if he'd spent the past year in the gym, or perhaps a dojo or boxing ring, getting out his frustrations in that most traditionally masculine of exercise: controlled violence.

Watching him now, Lola held her breath. Then he reached for her. Slowly, he pulled off her knee-high black boots, one after the other, tossing them to the floor with a noisy skitter of leather against tile.

Climbing beside her on the bed, he leaned forward to kiss her. She wrapped her arms around the warmth of his skin, feeling the hard muscles of his back.

He lifted her arms over her head and pulled off her shirt, revealing the black lace bra that barely contained her full breasts.

His expression was savage. Lowering his head, he kissed her lips hungrily. As his mouth moved slowly down her throat, she gripped his bare shoulders, closing her eyes, letting her head fall back against the pillow. He kissed her collarbone, and then lower, as his hands cupped her breasts over the black lace. He slowly caressed down her body, to her waist, to her belly and the edge of her black leggings.

He pulled the fabric slowly down her legs. She felt the butterfly-soft stroke of his fingertips move over her thighs, to her knees and calves, all the way to the hollows of her feet. He tossed the leggings aside, leaving her spread on the bed in only her bra and panties.

He looked at her, his expression dark.

"You're mine now, Lola," he said in a low voice. "To do with as I please."

She leaned up to cup his rough, angular cheek. "And you're mine…"

Reaching up, she kissed him, softly, seductively, swirling her tongue against his. She heard his soft groan.

With a low growl, he pushed her back against the bed, covering her body with his own. Reaching behind her, he unhooked her bra with a flick of his thumb, dropping the flimsy lace to the floor.

A choking sound came from the back of his throat when he saw her full, naked breasts. He gently cupped each one in awe, before kissing the valley between them to the soft slope of her belly, flicking her belly button gently with his tongue. His hands gripped her hips as his head moved lower.

She closed her eyes, her breath coming in ragged gasps as he kissed her skin along the top edge of her black lace panties, then, soft and slow, he pulled the lace down her hips, down her thighs, and took them off entirely.

She was naked in his bed, in a golden glow of light, with the windows open and the warm salt air breezes blowing in from the ocean.

Slowly, he spread her legs apart, kneeling between them. As he lowered his head, she felt the heat of his breath between her thighs. His fingertips slowly stroked up her hips, reaching around to grasp her backside.

Closing her eyes, she held her breath as he bent to taste her.

He slowly, ruthlessly, possessed her with his lips and tongue. She gasped with the intensity of pleasure as he splayed her wide with his hands, first lapping her, then moving the tip of his tongue around her taut nub in a sensual swirl that sent her higher and higher, until her whole body panted for release, and her hips started to lift off the bed.

When he lifted his head, she looked at him, and saw his black eyes glittering with feral need. In a single movement, he pulled off his trousers and black silk boxers.

She reached up her arms to him in silent demand. He moved up, and she felt his hard shaft between her thighs.

Then, as their eyes locked, he slowly pushed himself inside her.

She gasped as he filled her, inch by delicious inch. She gripped his shoulders, feeling him deep inside her, and hard, so hard. Slowly, he pulled back to thrust again, even deeper this time. She started to tremble as pleasure drew her back in a wave so high it threatened to drown her.

He rode her harder, faster. She held her breath, feeling dizzy as joy lifted her higher and higher still. Until suddenly, as he filled her to the hilt, pleasure exploded inside her, flinging her past the sky, into the stars.

CHAPTER FOUR

RODRIGO LOOKED DOWN at Lola as she cried out with pleasure, her face incandescent with joy. He gripped her shoulders, barely keeping himself from exploding into her.

He'd thought he could keep his distance, to make this about their bodies, only about sex. He was wrong. It wasn't just her body.

It was her face. Her voice. It was her.

Lola.

The only one he'd wanted. The one he'd dreamed about for the last year, in hot, unwilling dreams. Every morning, he'd woken up, still aching for her.

Now, at last, she was his. Forever.

And you're mine, she'd said.

Her claim washed through his soul. He trembled. He gloried in his possession of her.

But he could not surrender in his turn. Could not give himself fully. Not to Lola, or any woman.

But his hands were shaking as he gripped her. When he saw her burst with pleasure, a rush went through his body, through his soul, with a pounding roar.

Cupping her face in his hands, he said urgently, "You're mine forever. You'll never betray me. Say it."

"I'll never betray you," she said breathlessly, her beautiful face rosy with passion, her half-lidded eyes bright with ecstasy. And he believed her.

Lowering his lips against hers, he felt a searing joy—almost like pain—as his heart cracked inside him, like steel in sparks of flame. He wanted to trust her. He wanted to. She was his wife now. His—

And in that moment, for the first time in his life, Rodrigo lost control.

Gripping her hips, he gave in to the pleasure punching through him with violent force, knocking out his breath. A low growl built into a roar as he shattered, shuddering as he poured himself inside her.

And he collapsed.

When Rodrigo finally came back to awareness, it could have been minutes or hours later. He found himself tenderly holding her body against his own. Their bodies were intertwined, and he saw the warm, fading glow of twilight.

As he held Lola in his arms, joy went through him. It was as if the last miserable year had just been a bad dream.

Then he saw the motes of dust moving lazily in the light, like flickers of gold floating softly to the floor. And he remembered—everything.

Remembered why he could never trust any woman.

Especially now. They were married. They had a child. There was too much at stake.

He couldn't let down his guard. Because every time he did…

Pain cut through him, even more overwhelming than the pleasure had been. Suddenly shaking, he withdrew his hands from where they'd rested so cozily, so tenderly, on her body.

Rodrigo had thought he could have sex with a cold heart. But the joke was on him. He'd thought he could take her like a conqueror. Instead, after a year of mutual hunger, she'd matched his fire, and they'd burned together like a phoenix rising to the sun. It hadn't just been physical, but almost holy.

Far from conquering her, he'd wanted to give her—everything.

Slowly getting out of bed, he silently backed away. But as he picked up his trousers and boxers from the tile floor, he heard her lilting, husky voice.

"Where are you going now?"

His spine snapped straight. He turned to face her.

"Out. I'm going out."

Frowning at his tone, she slowly sat up in bed. "Where?"

His gaze traced unwillingly on her soft skin, the smooth curves of her body now a soft pink in the fading sunlight. He kept his face expressionless, careful to give nothing away. He'd learned, while building his media empire, that any emotional weakness only invited destruction.

But he hadn't just learned it in business. He'd learned it long before. From every single woman he'd known.

He said shortly, "Where I go is none of your concern."

Her lips twisted. "Of course it is. I'm your wife."

"I have business."

"Where?"

He thought fast. "South America."

"What?" Lola sat up straight, her expression incredulous. "You can't be serious. You just dragged me to California!"

"My business cannot wait," he said, but the truth was, *he* couldn't wait. To be as far away from her as possible.

"We'll come with you, then." She lifted her chin. "You married me so we could be a family. So you could help raise our son. Our place is at your side."

He had said that, Rodrigo realized. Did she see what had changed? Could she see the sudden weakness in his soul? Ice filled his heart.

"Your place is where I say it is," he said harshly. "I won't have you dragging Jett around the world for no reason."

She drew her knees up against her chest. She looked

suddenly young and forlorn. "Then why did you bring us here? Just to leave us?"

Rodrigo stared down at her, his heart pounding. But he couldn't let himself bend. If he did, he might break. Making love to her had left him strangely vulnerable. The walls around his soul, normally impregnable, felt as brittle as untempered steel.

"I will return soon. In the meantime, Mrs. Lee can help with the baby. Tobias and Lester will guard the door and drive you anywhere you require."

"Don't go," she whispered, her hazel eyes luminous.

"You'll be fine." Looking into her beautiful face, all shadows and rosy light, Rodrigo came closer. He lowered his head to briefly kiss her lips. She was soft and warm in his arms. He felt his body start to respond.

Ripping away, he choked out, "I'll leave my credit cards. My checkbook. Buy anything you desire."

And he left, without looking back.

Lola didn't expect to miss him, but she did.

Over the next week, she tried to distract herself from his absence by busily settling in to the beach house and caring for their baby. She bought new clothes for both her and Jett, suitable for the warm California weather and sunny days on the beach or by the pool. She found a new pediatrician, and a wonderful baby boutique in Santa Monica. Rodrigo had told her to use his credit cards, so she'd done her best.

But her heart wasn't in it. Shopping felt lonely. Strange, since she was never alone. Rodrigo's bodyguards, Tobias and Lester, insisted on driving Lola wherever she needed to go, and accompanied her and the baby whenever they left the compound. Even back at the beach house, kindly, warm Mrs. Lee was there all day, keeping the house in order and puttering in the kitchen, always offering to help or chat.

But Lola wasn't feeling chatty. The enormous, luxurious beach house had lost its shine. She felt Rodrigo's absence every day.

And every night.

Lola wasn't a romantic like her friend Tess. She had no dreams of hearts and flowers. But having her husband disappear after one day of marriage was beneath even her low expectations.

The big diamond ring weighed heavily on her left hand. Whenever she looked at it, it seemed to glitter back at her hollowly.

What kind of stupid marriage was this?

Lola tried to tell herself she didn't care. After all, she wasn't the one who'd demanded marriage. She and Jett had done fine without Rodrigo before. They could again.

She just wished if he'd changed his mind about their marriage that fast, he would tell her, so she and Jett could go back to New York, where they belonged. Where she had friends, people who would at least answer when she called!

Rodrigo only ignored her. Just that morning, Lola had gotten the thrilling news that she'd passed her GED, forwarded to California from her address in New York. Rodrigo had been the first one she'd wanted to tell. After all, he'd encouraged her, telling her she should have gone to college or even law school. Almost bouncing with excitement, she'd dialed his number.

But he didn't pick up his phone. Even after she called him multiple times. Finally, disconsolately, she texted him the news. He hadn't responded to that either.

Of course he hadn't. He'd given her the silent treatment all week, ignoring her calls, and even simple messages like her asking where things were in the house or if he'd already arranged a doctor for the baby. Even the message she'd sent him yesterday, informing him of the six-figure gift she planned for her baby sisters, had gotten no answer.

It was enough to make her hate this beautiful beach

house, where they'd once been so happy. And yearn to be somewhere else. Anywhere. But especially New York.

Wrapping her arms around herself, drawing her cashmere cardigan closer, Lola looked out the wall of windows overlooking the pool and, beyond that, the ocean and sky.

The sun was golden and warm, just like it had been the day Rodrigo brought her back here as his bride. He'd looked at her with so much emotion in his dark eyes before he'd kissed her. He'd made love to her with such fire and heat, such explosive pleasure, even more spectacular than she'd felt during their affair. She'd looked up into his handsome face as his body covered hers, and for one moment, she'd imagined their marriage could be about more than duty.

But obviously, she'd thought wrong. Because when Rodrigo had gotten up from the bed, he'd looked at her as if he hated the sight of her. And ever since, he'd ignored her, as if she were Typhoid Mary and he was afraid he might contract her disease from wherever he was in South America. If he really was in South America.

What had she done, to make him suddenly want to not only leave the bed but leave the continent?

Tess and Hallie would know, she thought suddenly. Hallie was always so sensible and practical, while Tess was idealistic with those rose-colored glasses. Missing them, she felt a lump in her throat. She'd sent them messages about her GED, and unlike her husband they'd immediately called, to cheer for her.

"Lola, you're so sneaky!" Hallie had said. "You never even told us you dropped out of high school when you were a kid!"

"You should have told us you were working for your GED," Tess chided. "I could have baked you cookies to help you study!"

Lola smiled now, thinking about them. Then her smile faded. What would Tess and Hallie say when they learned she'd left New York without telling them, and now lived in California? What would they say when they learned the identity of Jett's father, and that Lola had married him without inviting them to the wedding?

She should have told them, when they were congratulating her for passing her GED. She'd tried to. But the words had stuck in her throat. She wasn't like her friends, wanting to talk and talk about their unsolved problems.

Lola solved her own problems. *Then* she'd talk about them.

And the problem of her marriage felt very much unsolved. How could she explain why she'd married Rodrigo and moved to California at his demand, only for him to promptly dump her and Jett here and disappear?

Suddenly, Lola narrowed her eyes. She'd tried to be patient. But she'd had enough of waiting and wondering.

Any action was better than this.

He'd told her to spend his money? Fine. She would.

Going into Rodrigo's home office, she found his checkbook and wrote out a six-figure check, which she signed with a flourish. Anger made her fearless. Getting an envelope and paper, she wrote a letter to her sisters, the first time she'd written them in seven years.

Seven. She'd never meant to fall out of her sisters' lives so completely. But the days had passed so fast. Already, Johanna was twelve, and Kelsey was fifteen. *Fifteen.* The same age Lola had been when her mother died. When she'd decided to make it her life's mission to save her family.

She'd failed then. But maybe, if her little sisters knew how hard she'd tried, they would forgive her. And this check couldn't hurt, either.

With a deep breath, Lola signed the letter and tucked it into the envelope with the check. Sealing it, she wrote the address she'd long ago memorized by heart.

Her hand shook as she left the home office. Collecting

Jett from his playpen in the sunny main room, where he'd been happily chewing on toys, she felt so elated at what she'd done, she sang him a song she used to sing to her sisters. The baby giggled and cooed as she danced with him, pausing to look out through the windows at the bright blue ocean and sky.

Then she stopped. What if it didn't work? What if her sisters ignored her, just like Rodrigo?

Squaring her shoulders, Lola forced herself to go into the enormous, gleaming kitchen, where she found the housekeeper taking bread out of the oven. It smelled delicious.

"I made your favorite, Mrs. Cabrera," Mrs. Lee said, smiling. "I know how much you love it."

"You're too good to me. I was, um, wondering…" Lola nervously held up the envelope. "Is there any way you could take this to the post office? I'd do it myself but…" *But I'm scared I'll chicken out.*

"I'd be happy to." Wiping her hands on her apron, the older woman took the envelope with a smile. "I have a bunch of errands to run this morning anyway. Shall I do it now?"

"Yes, please, if you don't mind. And please get a tracking number and receipt."

"Oh, my." Mrs. Lee tilted her head. "It sounds important."

"It is. It's a present. For my…my sisters." Lola's heart was beating fast. She knew the girls were happy in their adoptive family. She'd long ago given up thoughts of custody. All she wanted now was for her sisters to remember her. And maybe, if she was very lucky, to forgive her. "Thank you, Mrs. Lee."

After the housekeeper was gone, Lola changed into a modest swimsuit and cover-up, put a swimsuit on the baby and slathered him with sunscreen, and put hats on them both to block out the hot California sun. Carrying Jett with one arm, and a large wicker basket full of toys with the other, she struggled out onto the white sand. Stretching out a beach blanket, she set up her baby comfortably, then sat down beside him.

With a deep breath, Lola stared out at the wide blue ocean stretching out to the west, all the way to Hawaii and Japan. She wanted to call back Mrs. Lee, and tell her not to send the letter. She felt scared and alone. Would her sisters ever forgive her?

But as she reached for her phone to call back Mrs. Lee, she heard Rodrigo's firm words.

You know how to argue people into things. When you're ready to see your sisters, you'll figure out how.

With a deep breath, she put down her phone. She'd try to be strong.

She wondered where Rodrigo was at this moment.

Staring out at the horizon, she saw something out of the corner of her eye. Turning, she saw a man coming toward her on the beach. For a moment, she thought it was Rodrigo. But it was a stranger. It was so unexpected, she sat up straight on the beach blanket, blinking in surprise.

A stranger? On this beach?

All of California's beaches were public, at least in theory, but this beach was virtually private, as it was on an isolated inlet surrounded by cliffs to the north and south.

The man looked like a surfer, wearing board shorts, flip-flops and an unbuttoned shirt that showed off his hard-muscled chest. He had blond hair, a deep tan and a toothy smile.

"Hello," she said, frowning.

"Hello," he said, smiling down at her. "Are you all alone? You're too beautiful to be lonely. Would you like some company? You and your charming baby?"

Lola's mouth dropped. Was this stranger hitting on her? She wasn't wearing a bikini but a modest cover-up. But he was looking at her as if he were a cat and she was a fish. For the first time, she wished the bodyguards were around.

"No, thanks." Picking up Jett from the blanket, she quickly packed up her things in the wicker basket. "I was just leaving."

"You were?" he said, his tanned face disappointed.

"Sorry." Straightening her big sun hat, she carried the baby and wicker basket back to the house, walking swiftly. Once she reached the safety of the terrace, she turned to look back. The beach was empty. The stranger was gone.

Of course he was. Lola exhaled. Obviously, she'd been alone in this house too long, to get so weirded out just by someone being friendly. Or maybe she'd finally become a true New Yorker. Strangers talking to her made her suspicious and alarmed.

But still, she couldn't shake the uneasy feeling.

Inside the beach house, she went to find the bodyguards. Lester was nowhere to be found, but she discovered Tobias pacing angrily in the courtyard, speaking into his cell phone.

"Chelsea, what are you talking about?" He gripped his phone. "You know I'm supposed to have him. This is the third time you've brushed me off." He listened, then an expletive escaped his lips. "That's a lie and you know it. He doesn't have homework. He's five! I deserve to see my son. And he deserves it, too. I pay child support. I've tried to be patient, but we both know the real reason…"

Tobias saw Lola, and his face went pale. "I have to call you back," he said, then scowled, "No, Chelsea, *tonight*. And if you even think you…"

Coming forward, Lola calmly plucked the phone out of his hand. "Hello, this is Mrs. Cabrera. Tobias's employer."

"So?" the woman's voice was sour, ready for battle. Good, because that was exactly Lola's mood.

"If you don't let him see his son, which is apparently

his legal right, we're going to have to either let him go, which means you'll be getting no more child support, or else we'll consider sending a full team of LA's best lawyers to ask the judge to reopen the case and pursue full custody on his behalf."

"What do you care?" the woman bit out.

"I don't," Lola said coolly. "But he's supposed to be protecting us, and it's obvious he can't do that when he's so distressed. Why won't you allow him to see his son?"

"None of your business!"

"But it is, as I just explained. So what's it to be? No more money? Or back to court?"

Silence fell on the other end.

"My new boyfriend doesn't like Tobias coming around."

"I understand," Lola said, relaxing. "But your son is the most important thing. Right? And your son needs his father. Doesn't he?"

There was a grudging sigh. "Yes," the woman said finally. She paused. "Fine. I'll deal with my boyfriend. Mason misses his father, too. He's been complaining about it. Put Tobias back on."

Lola handed the phone to Tobias. "Here."

Satisfaction flashed through her as she headed back into the house, carrying her baby on her hip. At least she hadn't lost all her skills. After unpacking her beach bag, she gave Jett a bath to wash off all the sunscreen. She toweled him off, changed him into fresh clothes and then held him close, relishing the clean baby smell.

Afterward, she carried him back toward the kitchen, intending to make herself a comforting cup of tea. Tobias was waiting for her in the great room.

"I get to see my son tonight after work," he said. "My ex is even going to give me extra time, to make up for the days I missed." He shook his head. "How did you talk her into it?"

She shrugged. "It wasn't hard."

"I guess the real question," he said slowly, "is why did you get involved?"

"As I said, I wanted your full attention—"

"Mrs. Cabrera." Shaking his head, he gave her a grin. "How dumb do you think I am?"

She stared at him, unblinking. Then she said slowly, "My father died when I was five, the same age as your son. I have almost no memories of him." She looked away. "I hate it when families are separated."

"I see," Tobias said quietly. He paused. "Was there some reason you came looking for me earlier?"

Sitting here, in this elegant, luxurious beach house, her earlier fears about the stranger on the beach seemed paranoid. "I just wondered if you'd heard from my husband since he left. Because...because I haven't. He hasn't answered any of my calls." At his astonished expression, she said quickly, "I just want to know Rodrigo is okay."

Tobias stared at her, then held out his phone. "Try calling him with this."

Lola's eyes went wide. She looked up at him. "Are you sure?"

He shrugged.

"He might fire you," she said.

"He can try." Tobias gave a crooked grin. "But I'm backing you, Mrs. Cabrera."

"Thank you," she whispered.

He turned away. Lola stared down at the bodyguard's phone in her hand. Slowly, she typed in Rodrigo's name. His number came up.

Taking a deep breath, she hit the dial button.

An hour after Rodrigo's private jet landed in Los Angeles, he walked into his office building downtown, feeling exhausted in a way that had nothing to do with his hectic business travel to his bustling film studio in Mexico City or his newly acquired television network in Buenos Aires.

For the last week, he'd barely slept. Even when he had, peace had evaded him. And he knew why.

Because of *her*.

He'd taken Lola as his wife. Taken her to his bed. He now had her securely under his control, and at a distance. He hadn't answered any of her messages or calls. He got reports on her welfare, and that of his son, from his bodyguards. He'd thought that would create the emotional distance he needed.

So why did Rodrigo still feel so vulnerable?

Why did he dream of Lola every night, in sensual dreams that were even worse than before?

Why did he wake up gasping for her like a suffocating man struggling desperately for breath?

He didn't have control of her, damn it. He didn't even have control of himself. It was why he'd left. Why he hadn't wanted to let himself be near her. Why he couldn't bear to look at her or hear her voice.

Lola made him want. She made him *feel*.

And feeling anything for a woman always led to loss. Women were liars. Deceivers. They couldn't be trusted, except to cause pain.

Keeping his distance was the only way this marriage would work. The only way to give his child a stable family and home.

But even being thousands of miles away hadn't created the distance he'd wanted. He had to find another solution. Because Lola was right. He hadn't dragged her to the altar just to abandon her and neglect his child.

Being away from his tiny son for a week had been intolerable. And Rodrigo knew Lola. She wouldn't put up with this silent treatment forever. Honestly, he was surprised she hadn't already tried to revolt.

Setting his jaw, he strode into his private office and tossed his briefcase carelessly on his gleaming dark wood desk. Turning, he looked out the windows overlooking the skyscrapers and haze of downtown Los Angeles.

Sleeping with Lola hadn't gotten her out of his system. For the last week, as he'd made deals, the image of her soft and rosy in bed, the memory of her body against his own, had fogged his brain in a hum of desire. He wanted her. In bed. On his desk. Against the wall. He wanted to possess her until they were both utterly satiated, however long that took. Even if it took forever.

But how could he make love to her, without being tempted to care?

"You're back!" Turning, he saw his executive assistant, Marnie McAdam, standing in the doorway. "Here are your messages, Mr. Cabrera." Setting down a small pile on his desk, she cleared her throat. "The International Studio Guild wants to know if you're bringing your wife to Madrid."

Rodrigo had the sudden vision of appearing with Lola on his arm, in all her rapturous beauty, when he accepted the award in Madrid next week for CEO of the Year. He'd be envied for his wife, even more than the prestigious award. And afterward, he'd take her to his bed and…

He shivered inside.

"I haven't thought about it," he said shortly.

"You need a date. It's a social event." Marnie tilted her head, looking at him owlishly through her glasses. "If she can't come, I could do it. Not as a date or anything," she added hastily, "but, you know, just to help out."

Rodrigo frowned at his assistant. Bring her to the ceremony? What was Marnie talking about?

Then he saw her pale, determined expression and relaxed. Marnie wasn't flirting with him, *gracias a Dios*. She was merely trying to solve a logistical problem on his behalf, like any good secretary would. "Thank you," he said smoothly, "but such a sacrifice on your part won't be necessary."

"It would be no problem, truly—"

"I know you don't care to travel. I'll deal with it."

Yes, by bringing Lola to Madrid, his body suggested slyly.

Perhaps he was taking it all too seriously, Rodrigo thought suddenly. Perhaps the emotional reaction he'd had last week had been a one-time thing, caused by his year of wanting her.

He blinked.

Sí, it was possible. In which case, the only way to prevent it from happening again was to take Lola to bed and binge on her until he was cured, like someone who, after drinking whiskey until he's sick, can never bear to taste it again.

Yes. The more that he thought of this—

His phone rang from his pocket. Looking down, he saw the call was from one of his bodyguards, Tobias.

"That'll be all for now, Marnie." He nodded at her. As she closed the door behind her, he answered his phone. "Is my wife becoming a problem?"

"I'm your problem now."

Her low voice made electricity skitter through his body, even as his spine snapped straight.

"Lola." He breathed deeply. "How did you get this phone?"

"I had no choice, did I? You're clearly not interested in taking my calls."

Rodrigo exhaled, and kept his voice a cold, deliberate drawl. "I've been traveling for business—"

"When I married you, Rodrigo, I meant it to be forever. But forever's not going to be like this."

And the phone went dead in his hands.

CHAPTER FIVE

WHEN RODRIGO ARRIVED at the beach house, Lola was ready for a fight.

She'd already packed her clothes and the baby's. Because she knew an ultimatum always came at a price—of possibly being forced to go through with the threat.

But she hadn't married him to be abandoned. If Rodrigo didn't intend to actually fulfill his promise to be a good father to their baby, then Lola was taking Jett back to New York, to be around people who actually cared about them. Marriage required two people, not just one.

When Rodrigo burst through the door, he strode into the great room, darkly handsome and a little terrifying. Lola faced him defiantly, holding their baby in her arms.

As usual, he was dressed entirely in black, even in sunny California. Unlike Lola, who now wore a T-shirt and shorts suitable for the weather, Rodrigo never changed, no matter where he was or what country he was in. He expected the world to conform to him, not the other way around.

Sometimes she'd liked that about him, that he was steadfast and strong, like an oak in a world full of weeds. Today wasn't one of those times.

"Nice of you to visit," Lola said coldly. "I thought maybe you'd forgotten you were married. Maybe you do need a ring."

He dropped his briefcase with a bang on the floor, causing their baby to jump with surprise in her arms. "I was *traveling*. For *business*."

She juggled Jett on her hip. "You got here fast, at least."

"I arrived in LA this morning. I was at the office when you called."

It surprised her how much that hurt. "You went there first? Instead of home?"

"Business comes first. You know that."

"Over family?"

"You were fine. You had Tobias and Lester and Mrs. Lee."

Lola glared at him. "You're seriously not this stupid."

He looked at her incredulously. "Stupid?"

"Is this your idea of marriage, of family, to just dump us and disappear? Because it's not what I signed up for."

Rodrigo looked irritated. "It's only been a week."

"Our first week. Our *honeymoon*."

"Don't be ridiculous, Lola." His dark eyes glittered. "We're not in love. Our marriage isn't based on romance."

"It should at least be based on respect. We have to look out for each other." She lifted her chin. "Otherwise, what's the point?"

Rodrigo scowled, then turned away, staring out the wide windows toward the infinite blue water of the Pacific.

Lola took a deep breath. "Look, if you want out of this marriage—"

"I don't," he said, cutting her off.

"Are you sure?" She set her jaw. "Because I've packed my bags. If you're just going to ignore me, I'm taking Jett back to New York. To be with friends."

Rodrigo slowly reached out to stroke Jett's hair. Then his dark eyes met hers. "You're right. I never should have left."

She sucked in her breath. She hadn't realized until that moment how tense she'd been. She hadn't expected Rodrigo to admit fault. He never had before.

"I'll never abandon you like that again, Lola," he said quietly. "I give you my word."

Lola felt a strange sensation in her chest. She'd been so ready for the worst. She cleared her throat. "Oh. Well, good." Her voice was a little hoarse. "We're supposed to be a family."

"I want that, too."

They stared at each other for a long moment. Then she turned away.

"Jett's started to get a tooth, did you see?" Lola pointed at his mouth. The baby, now four and a half months old, was cuddled against her hip, babbling happily to himself as he tried to chew on his pudgy hand. "That's why he's drooling. Yesterday, he rolled over for the first time. And he's gained another pound. His pediatrician says he's doing great."

"Look at you, *pequeño*," Rodrigo said, putting his hand on the baby's back. As he moved, his fingertips briefly brushed the bare skin of Lola's arm. Electricity went through her.

"You missed so much," she whispered. "I wrote to my sisters."

"Yes. You sent the gift?"

"Yes."

"You said how much it cost," he said dryly. "You didn't say what it was. A new house?"

The corners of her lips lifted. "I promised to pay for the entirety of their college educations. Medical school, law school, anything they want, at any university in the world."

His eyes widened. Then he smiled. "Very nice."

"And I passed my GED." In spite of her best efforts, hurt filled her voice. "I sent you a message. I wanted you to be proud of me."

"I was proud. I knew you could do it."

"But you ignored me!"

"I told Marnie to arrange flowers. Didn't she send them?"

Her eyes narrowed. "No. She didn't."

His jaw, dark with a five o'clock shadow, tightened. "You need to get over your irrational hatred for her, Lola."

Her eyes went wide. "Irrational!"

"She thought I had the right to know about your past. Both as your employer and as your lover."

"She's a smug know-it-all!" Lola thought of all the times Marnie had put her down for her lack of education, implying she wasn't smart enough for her job. "She wasn't doing it for your sake. She was trying to get rid of me!"

His expression shuttered. "Stop blaming her for your own bad choices. She's not the one with half-naked pictures, or who tried to sell herself at eighteen to be a star."

"I never tried to sell myself!" Lola cried, her hands tightening on her baby, who was fidgeting in her arms.

Rodrigo looked at her incredulously. "I saw the pictures. Why won't you admit the rest?"

Pain burst through her. She turned away, trembling. Carefully, she set Jett down in his baby play gym, leaving him to batt happily at colorful dangling toys. Taking a deep breath, she counted to ten. Then she faced Rodrigo.

"I didn't try to sell myself to be a star," she said in a low voice. "I was just desperate for money."

He snorted. "If you think that sounds better—"

"Just shut up a minute, will you!"

He fell silent. Her hands clenched at her sides.

"I told you my sisters and I were split up into foster care…" Her voice trailed off as she remembered how, at fifteen, with her mother dead and her stepfather gone, the social workers had pulled her from her half sisters, then only five and three. The little girls had cried and screamed, clinging to Lola, begging her not to let them go. Their screams haunted Lola for the next three years.

"Yes?" he said.

She shook her head. "I promised I'd get them back as soon as I could, so we could be a family again. The day I turned eighteen, I dropped out of high school and moved to LA hoping to make enough money. My plan was to be a movie star. I failed."

"Most actors do fail," he said matter-of-factly.

"I know that now." She flashed him a tremulous smile. "Plus, you know what a bad liar I am. I couldn't act my way out of a paper bag. I'd always been told I was pretty, but Los Angeles is full of pretty girls. Then I met a man who said he was an agent, and could make me a star. I let him take pictures of me in lingerie. He said they were test shots."

Folding his arms, Rodrigo was silent, watching her. Not meeting his eyes, Lola forced herself to continue.

"He sent me to a hotel suite, supposedly to meet with a producer. But the man didn't even bother letting me read for the part." Her cheeks went hot. "He tried to rip off my clothes and hold me down on the bed."

Rodrigo growled. Looking up, she saw waves of fury visible around him, from his tight shoulders and hard eyes.

"I kicked him in the groin and ran from the hotel room. He shouted after me that I'd never work in Hollywood again." She looked down at the floor. "And I didn't."

Rodrigo came toward her. "I'm sorry."

She swallowed hard, imagining she saw pity in his eyes. "Marnie must have spoken with my old agent to get the photographs. But she got the story wrong. I never tried to seduce anyone for a role." She gave a low laugh, wiping her eyes. "In fact, the whole experience was so awful I avoided being alone with men for years. Until—" She lifted her gaze.

His dark eyes burned through her. "Until me?"

She lowered her head. "Later, I almost wished I'd just

given the man what he wanted. Because by the time I earned enough as a secretary, it was too late."

"Too late?"

Lola turned away, toward the great room's windows. For a moment, she stared out past the terrace and slender palm trees toward the white sand and blue ocean. "Too late to get my family back."

Her heart hurt as she remembered how, after she'd finally earned enough to get her own apartment without roommates, she'd rushed to visit her sisters, to tell them they could all finally be together. She'd been nearly weeping with joy and relief.

But she found Kelsey and Johanna, now nine and six, pedaling gleaming new bikes on a perfect street in front of a new two-story house in the LA suburbs, as their golden retriever bounded in the sunshine.

"What happened?" Rodrigo said.

"They didn't remember me," Lola said in a low voice. "When I told them I'd be taking them to come live with me, they started crying and clung to their foster mother. The woman started yelling at me. And I found out—"

"Found out?"

"My stepfather had already relinquished his parental rights from prison." Her shoulders sagged. "They'd just been permanently adopted by their foster family." She took a deep breath. "I started yelling and crying. The parents were so scared of me, they moved away. To New York."

"Lola," he said softly.

Suddenly, she couldn't hold back her tears.

"I lost my family, Rodrigo," she choked out. "I failed."

For the first time in her adult life, she let someone see her cry, not a pretty cry either, but ugly and raw. Without a word, Rodrigo pulled her into his strong arms. For long moments, he just held her, stroking her hair as she wept against his shirt.

Finally, her sobs faded. Silence fell. With her cheek pressed against his chest, she could feel the steady, comforting beat of his heart.

"You didn't fail them, Lola," he said in a low voice. "You tried your best, when you were barely more than a kid yourself. You need to stop blaming yourself." He gently kissed the top of her head. "You'll hear from them soon."

Drawing back, she said breathlessly, "You think so?"

"Definitely." He gave her a crooked grin. "After the present you gave them, I don't see how they could resist."

Wiping her eyes, she gave a small laugh, like a sob.

Reaching out, he cupped her cheek. "And you have a new family now," he whispered. "Jett." His eyes met hers. "Me."

Their eyes locked. "You're my family?"

"I want to be," he said quietly, then shook his head. "Obviously I'm not very good at it. But I've never had one before."

"What are you talking about? You had parents. You were rich. You inherited a fortune—"

A flash of emotion crossed his hard, handsome face, but was quickly veiled. "Being wealthy isn't always what it's cracked up to be."

Rodrigo had been hurt, too, she realized. Somehow, in his childhood, he'd been hurt. Her arms tightened protectively around him in turn.

"We have to look out for each other," she said. "Watch each other's backs. Just like we used to, when we worked together. Do you remember?"

"You and me against the world?" She nodded, and his dark eyes flickered. "Remember what you said the first day you came to work for me?"

A whisper of a smile traced her lips. "I said you were a disaster and you'd hired me just in the nick of time."

"It was true. Since you left, my company hasn't done nearly as well. Neither have I."

"You have Marnie," she said, striving to keep the bitterness from her voice.

He shook his head. "She's had to hire two extra assistants just to keep up with what you did on your own. She's loyal and tries hard, but she doesn't have your skill. People still ask for you. You always remembered everything." Looking down at her, he said softly, "I miss you. I achieved more with you at my side."

"I'm back at your side now."

"You're right," he said slowly. He took a deep breath, then said humbly, "I have a business trip next week to Madrid. Would you come with me? You and Jett?"

Lola put down her arms, looking uncertain. "Madrid?"

Rodrigo tried to look modest. "I'm getting the award for CEO of the Year from the International Studio Guild."

It was an incredibly prestigious award. She sucked in her breath in delight. "You are?"

Reaching out, he tucked a tendril of blond hair behind her ear. "You're a big reason for it."

She tried not to tremble at his touch. "Me?"

Rodrigo gave a nod. "You helped me organize and acquire a television network that now stretches around the Pacific Rim, from Tierra del Fuego to Alaska to Manila. You're the one who convinced me to produce a film no one else wanted, which cost almost nothing to make but has now made almost half a billion dollars worldwide."

Her eyes were big. *"The Sapphire Sea?"*

"Turns out that romance is back in style."

Her lips lifted. "Who knew?"

"So will you be my date?"

Lola paused. "Sure."

"Good," he said quietly. Hearing a loud, noisy yawn, he looked at their baby in his baby play gym. Then he looked back at Lola, and they both laughed.

"It's time for his nap," she said.

"Let me do it."

She hesitated, then nodded. Reaching down, he lifted the baby gently into his powerful arms.

"You missed your *papá* this week, didn't you, *pequeñito*?" he said tenderly, looking down at Jett.

Seeing the two of them together, the tiny baby held against Rodrigo's powerful chest, caused Lola's heart to twist. She quickly turned away before he could see new tears in her eyes. Really, all this crying was getting out of hand. What was wrong with her? Had she gone completely soft?

"Here's his blanket," she said, pulling it from her nearby diaper bag. "There's a bottle already in the fridge. I usually rock him to sleep—"

"We'll be fine," he said, still smiling down at the baby. But as he carried Jett toward the hallway, he stopped and looked back at her in the beach house's great room. "And, Lola?"

"Yes?"

"Thank you for trusting me." For a moment, his dark eyes glowed at her, tender and warm, then he turned back to the baby in his arms, and disappeared down the hall.

Standing in the shadows, Lola stood still. She felt her heart thudding painfully in her chest. Her cheeks were hot. She felt vulnerable, exposed. She'd never shared the story of her past before, with anyone. But then, Rodrigo wasn't just anyone. Not anymore.

Then, slowly, a smile lifted to her face.

They were a *family*.

A week later, Rodrigo smiled at his wife in the back seat of the Rolls-Royce as their Spanish chauffeur and bodyguard drove them through the streets of Madrid.

Her beautiful face lit up with pleasure as she pointed out the sights to their baby in the car seat between them, while their chauffeur drove them down the wide Calle de Alcalá. Lola had always loved Madrid when she'd come here as his assistant. Now, as he looked at her joyful face, everything felt new. For both of them.

He'd been wrong about so much. When he thought of the way he'd tossed her out of his life so ruthlessly last year, he felt almost ashamed. He should have asked Lola for an explanation, rather than just believing the worst of Marnie's report.

Trust didn't come easy for him, it was true. Mostly because every single time he'd trusted someone, they'd betrayed him.

But this was different. He'd known Lola for years. He should have given her the benefit of the doubt.

He'd make it up to her, Rodrigo told himself now. He'd watch out for her and give her the life she deserved. The life they both deserved.

A shudder went through him at the memory of the pleasures they'd shared over the past week. Their relationship had only intensified after Lola—tough, fearless Lola—had cried in his arms.

From that moment, all he'd known was that he had to protect her. She was a part of him now, and he never wanted to let her go.

He'd had her story checked out, of course. Trust, but verify. It was the best he could do. Women had lied to him too often, and though he'd believed her, he'd needed proof. There was knowing, and knowing.

But if anything, his investigator had told him, she'd downplayed the poverty and tragedy of her childhood. She'd left out the fact that her stepfather had gone to prison, then died there a few years later. She'd left out the fact that the illness of her mother could have been cured, if only she'd had money and time to see a specialist earlier.

And while the investigator was at it, Rodrigo had had

him check to see if Lola had had contact with any other men, especially Sergei Morozov. She hadn't.

Rodrigo could trust her. Really trust her.

It was a shock to his system. He couldn't remember the last time he'd really trusted anyone.

But it had turned out, though his wife had grown up in poverty in the California desert, and Rodrigo had grown up in luxury in Madrid, they weren't so different after all. They'd both been hurt.

But never again.

Rodrigo's eyes caressed his wife's beautiful face as she happily pointed out sights to their baby through the streets of Madrid.

They were a family.

The Rolls-Royce pulled to the curb in front of an elegant nineteenth-century building in the exclusive Salamanca district, on a wide, tree-lined avenue overlooking the vast green expanse of the Parque del Buen Retiro. As the driver opened the passenger door, Lola unbuckled their baby from the car seat. Getting out of the vehicle, she looked up in awe.

"It's actually finished?" she breathed.

"*Sí*. Finally." For most of his adult life, he'd avoided this building, preferring to stay at a luxury hotel like the Campania Madrid, rather than face his childhood home. It was Lola who'd convinced him, two years before, to remodel the place and make it his own. She'd been aghast at the thought that he'd allowed a nineteenth-century penthouse on the Calle de Alcalá, overlooking the famous park, to dilapidate into dust.

"I can't wait to finally see inside," Lola said now, her eyes sparkling. "You never let me see it before."

Rodrigo looked up at the building as memories floated back to him of his childhood. He'd been lonely here, with his parents often gone. And when they were home, the house was filled with their screaming fights, slamming doors, his mother's taunts, his father's broken bottles smashed against the walls and the sour smell of expensive, wasted wine.

"Rodrigo? Is something wrong?"

Coming back to himself, he shook his head. "There wasn't much to see, after twenty years of neglect. Broken-down walls. Dust."

"I can imagine," she said quietly, looking at him.

A twinge went through him at the sympathy of her gaze. It was too close to pity, which implied weakness.

Lola reached for his hand, her eyes glowing and warm. "But everything is different now."

For a moment, Rodrigo was lost in her eyes. Then he pulled his hand away.

"Yes." He turned on the Madrid sidewalk. "Come see."

As the chauffeur and bodyguard lingered outside, getting their bags from the car, Rodrigo led her into the lobby. Hiding a smile, he turned to see her reaction.

Holding their baby, Lola looked with awe at the grandeur of the seven-story atrium, with the large oval staircase climbing all the way up, around each floor. Her steps slowed, then stopped, as she tilted her head back to look up at the stained-glass cupola crowning the top ceiling, beaming warm patterns of colored light against the marble floor.

"Wow," she breathed. "You paid for the lobby to be remodeled, as well?"

"I bought the whole building. I remodeled all the other apartments and sold them at a fat profit."

She glanced at him sideways. "Nice."

"This way."

Rodrigo led her to the new large elevator that had replaced the rickety birdcage elevator he remembered as a child. His nanny had often taken him to play in Retiro Park, when his parents' screaming became too loud. But usually the screaming was still going on when they returned, even hours later. They could always hear it before they even reached the top floor. So his nanny, looking stressed and sorry for him, would invent games allowing them to linger in the elevator.

Now, the gleaming silver door slid open silently, and they rode it to the top floor. There, they had a view of the entire atrium, stretching seven stories below. At the penthouse door, Rodrigo paused for a moment. He realized he was listening. But the apartment was silent now. No one was screaming or smashing glass.

His proud, aristocratic Spanish father—or at least, the man he'd believed to be his father—had been wealthy from birth, and bought a small Spanish movie studio, which was where he'd met Rodrigo's mother, a spoiled, much younger American actress. He'd loved her—been obsessed with her—but she'd never loved him, only his money. She'd enjoyed taunting him with her affairs. His father's rage had finally gotten the better of him, and he'd died of a stroke when Rodrigo was twenty-one. His mother had died a few years later, from a bad reaction to anesthesia during plastic surgery.

He'd never met the chauffeur who had supposedly sired him. The man had died when Rodrigo was just a child.

So many lies. So much deceit and rage. Rodrigo took a deep breath, closing his eyes.

"What's wrong?" Lola said cheerfully, coming up to the door. "Did you lose the key?"

He looked back at her. Jett's childhood would be so different. He was beginning to trust his wife as no one else. They had the same goals. They respected each other. And there was no messy emotion like love or jealousy to cloud anyone's judgment.

But he knew he'd never tell her about his childhood. There was no point. He wanted neither her sympathy nor her inevitable attempt at psychological analysis. There were some things a man dealt with better on his own.

And his past was in the past. Over. Forgotten.

"Don't worry." Reaching into his pocket, he held up the key. "I have it."

Pushing open the door to the penthouse apartment, he let Lola enter first, with the baby. As she passed him, Rodrigo's gaze traced hungrily over the lush curves of his wife's body.

Her eyes were wide as she looked around the elegant, minimalist apartment with its large windows and view of the park and much of Madrid, beneath the Spanish sky. "This was your childhood home?"

He remembered the screaming, the expensive clutter, the broken glass. "It didn't always look like this."

"But still." The edges of her lips lifted as she turned back to him. "You should have seen the place I grew up."

"A trailer," he said. "On the edge of the California desert."

Lola's hazel eyes went wide. Her beautiful face turned pale as she breathed, "How do you know that?"

He came closer. "I had to find out what was true."

"You had me investigated?" He heard cold anger beneath her voice. He shrugged.

"I had to know if I could trust you."

"And now?"

Reaching out, he pulled her into his arms.

"Now I do," he whispered, and he lowered his mouth ruthlessly to hers.

CHAPTER SIX

SINCE THEY WERE in Madrid the day before the awards ceremony, Rodrigo decided to visit the set of his company's new
prestige film, a historical drama-romance of the Spanish
Civil War currently being shot near the Plaza de Canalejas.

But even there, as he discussed the production's prog-
ress with the film's director, his eyes rarely strayed from
his wife.

He couldn't look away from her. The way her beautiful face lit up as she chatted with the cast and crew. The
warmth of her hazel eyes. The joy of her smile.

Lola was more beautiful than the star of any movie, he
thought. Her long, highlighted hair swayed over her shoulders, caressing the tops of her breasts. She was dressed
modestly, in her black coat and jeans that showed off her
shape. As she pushed the baby stroller, she seemed utterly
unaware of the fact that wherever she went, Rodrigo's eyes
followed her.

Every other man's, too.

As she walked, her curvy body moved so gracefully and
sensually, she seemed to be dancing to unheard music. Rodrigo frowned when he saw her speaking earnestly to the
star of the film, a famous Spanish actress whom Rodrigo
had once known well. *Very* well.

Ten years before, when Rodrigo was just twenty-seven—
in the first flush of success, having expanded the derelict

Madrid studio he'd inherited from his father to twenty employees, including Marnie McAdam—he'd been briefly engaged to Pia Ramirez.

He'd fallen in love with Pia before they'd even met, while watching her onscreen, where she'd played a poignant heroine who sacrificed everything for love before she died, nobly and beautifully, at the end of the film. Five years older than Rodrigo, she'd seemed equally lovestruck after their first date. Within two weeks, he'd proposed marriage, and she'd accepted.

A month later, he'd been anonymously sent photos of Pia naked in bed with a man he didn't recognize. Young and naive as he'd been then, it had nearly killed him.

Little had Rodrigo known that this pattern would be repeated twice more, with two other women. A quick engagement, followed by an equally swift betrayal. With photographs.

But a few months earlier, when the director had wanted to hire Pia for this film, Rodrigo hadn't tried to stop him. Pia was talented and, at forty-two, still a major draw at the international box office. His other two ex-fiancées also still worked in the movie industry, and he'd never tried to hurt their careers. If you blacklisted everyone who betrayed you in Hollywood, you'd have no one left to work with.

But now, as the director continued to talk anxiously about the film's dailies and bloating budget, Rodrigo barely listened. His eyes kept falling on his wife talking to his former fiancée. He wondered what the two women could be talking about so intently. Him? No, surely not. Why would they?

Rodrigo's gaze dropped to Lola's backside, her hips. The gentle curve of her waist. She drew him like honey. He could hardly wait to take her home and—

He watched Lola take her phone out of her coat pocket. Looking down at it, she read something and smiled. A warm, intimate smile. As if she had a wicked secret. Still smiling, she tucked the phone back in her pocket.

What message could make her smile like that?

Who had sent it?

A memory of her voice came back to him. *If you're just going to ignore me, I'm taking Jett back to New York. To be with friends.*

Friends? A trickle of ice went down his spine. Friends like Sergei Morozov?

Why would the man propose if he's never even slept with you? His question echoed in his memory, along with her answer.

Because he thinks it's the only way he can have me.

It's nothing, Rodrigo told himself firmly. *She hasn't been in contact with Morozov. I know she hasn't.*

So why did he feel so suddenly on edge?

He interrupted the director in the middle of the man's sentence. "Excuse me."

"Of course." The director looked shocked, as if no one had dared to be rude to him for a long time. Leaving without a glance, Rodrigo strode past the side lights and cameras to the edge of the set.

"Hello," he said shortly to Pia Ramirez, who had been married to another man for eight years now. They had three children, none of whom he'd met, but he knew about them, in the way that everyone knew everything in the insular world of television and film production.

The Spanish actress sobered. "Hello." She smiled at Lola. "I just met your new wife."

"I see that." He looked at Lola. "What have you been talking about?"

Her lovely face was blank. "Nothing in particular."

But Rodrigo thought Lola had a guilty expression. What was she hiding? He didn't like it.

He ground his teeth into a smile. "I'm done here. Shall we go?"

"Sure." Her voice was overly casual as she turned to tuck a blanket around their baby in the stroller. "Jett is hungry, anyhow."

"So am I," he said.

She fed the baby in their waiting Rolls-Royce, then they decided to have lunch at his favorite tapas bar in Salamanca, on the Calle de Serrano. Afterward, sending away the Rolls-Royce and driver, they walked home down the lovely, boutique-lined street, pushing the sleeping baby in his stroller on the beautiful, though chilly, November day.

As they walked, they spoke of inconsequential things, such as the recent nominees for Best Picture and Best Director, and the speech Rodrigo intended to make during tomorrow night's International Studio Guild awards ceremony. But as he tried to tell himself he was being paranoid, because he'd already decided he could trust her, he found himself growing increasingly on edge as he heard pings from her coat pocket, indicating she was getting more messages on her phone.

Messages she studiously ignored.

Messages she obviously did not want to read in front of him.

Trying to reason away his sudden irrational fear, he reminded himself about the prenuptial agreement. Lola would never cheat on him. She'd lose everything.

But the more pings he heard from her pocket, the more his nerves felt scraped raw.

At Rodrigo's suggestion, they stopped in a designer boutique so Lola could find a new dress for the awards ceremony. As she went to the private dressing room with an armful of gowns, he waited in a private sitting area, next to their sleeping baby, calming his nerves with a glass of good champagne given to him by the solicitous salesgirl. He was already anticipating seeing Lola in the gowns.

Then he heard the noises from her nearby dressing room.

The pings coming fast and furious from behind the curtain.

And he realized, with a sickening lurch, that Lola was secretly, frantically sending messages back to the person who'd made her smile.

Rising from the comfortable white leather sofa, he crossed four steps to her dressing room. Scowling, he yanked open the velvet curtain.

Turning, Lola gasped, instinctively covering her half-naked body with her arms. He had a swift glimpse of her full breasts barely covered by a lacy black bra, and flimsy black panties. Instantly his breathing was hard, and so was everything else.

Then he saw the phone in her hand.

His body went cold, his breathing steadied, and everything became clear again. Looking down at her, Rodrigo said, his voice like ice, "Who are you talking to on your phone?"

Lola suddenly seemed to forget she was naked. She straightened, dropping her arms. Clutching her phone behind her back, she lifted her chin. "None of your business."

It was like waving a red flag in front of a bull.

"None of my business?" His voice was dangerously quiet now. "You're my wife."

"Your wife." Her eyes glittered. "Not your prisoner."

"Give me your phone."

"No!"

Reaching around her with his powerful arms, he felt her soft, half-naked body brush his own. As her plump breasts were crushed against his chest, his gaze fell to her full, raspberry-red lips.

He heard her intake of breath. Watched as the tip of her

pink tongue nervously licked the corners of her mouth, before her white teeth tugged into the tender flesh of her lower lip. For a moment, he felt lost, dizzy with need.

Grimly, he shook off the blinding haze of desire and reached around her to snatch her phone from her hand.

"You are such a jerk!" she cried.

He expected the phone to be locked, and for him to have to demand her password. But to his surprise, it wasn't protected. He touched the screen, and instantly saw whom she'd been talking to.

Rodrigo's eyes widened. She hadn't been exchanging messages with Sergei Morozov, or any other man.

She'd been chatting with two women. One called Tess, the other Hallie.

He looked swiftly through the messages, then looked up, dumbfounded. "These are just your friends."

"Of course," Lola said angrily, snatching the phone back. "Who else would I be talking to?"

"Why did you try to hide the messages from me?"

"Because they're private. They're my friends, not yours!"

"No." Did she think he was that stupid? He glared down at her. "There's a reason."

She narrowed her eyes, then said resentfully, "Fine. I wanted to ask you later tonight. After I had the chance to butter you up. Fat chance of that now!"

"You can't butter me up," he said arrogantly. She snorted, then shook her head.

"My friends were worried, since they hadn't seen me around for a while. They went to my apartment and Mildred told them I went away with some man."

"Not just a man. Your husband."

She sighed. "I didn't share that part yet. They were shocked enough as it was. I just said you were an ex who'd come back into my life." She bit her lip. "They're dying to know more. Tess invited us to Thanksgiving dinner next Thursday. I want to go. And tell them everything in person."

Rodrigo looked at her blankly.

"You know Thanksgiving, right?" she said, with exaggerated patience.

"Of course," he said. "It's one of the most profitable film weekends of the year in the US."

She rolled her eyes. "It's also a time to be with friends. Family. Turkey and mashed potatoes. Football on TV? Does that ring any bells?"

"I know Thanksgiving," he said, annoyed. "My mother was American."

Her eyes lit up. "So you know how important it is to spend the day with the people you love."

"It's not that big a deal. My parents usually were away that day. With...friends." His mother typically went jet-setting with her current lover, while his father either lost himself in work or pursued her in a rage, depending on his mood. Pushing the memory aside, he said, "But my mother always told our cook to bake me something like turkey. Often it was Spanish chicken with saffron rice."

"You're kidding." Shock flashed through Lola's eyes. "Your parents left you alone on Thanksgiving?"

"Somehow I survived," he said dryly.

She shook her head decisively. "You deserve a real holiday."

"So you're offering to visit your friends in New York for my sake? Noble."

"All right, you got me. I want to see them. Selfishly." Lola put her hand on his shoulder. "I couldn't invite them to our wedding. I wanted so badly for them to be there. But now Tess and Stefano are hosting Thanksgiving at their new home. I want to spend the day in New York. Either with you—" she lifted her chin "—or without you."

For a moment, Rodrigo was distracted by her soft touch

against his arm, and the full view of her breasts as she looked up at him with defiant hazel eyes. His blood quickened. "You're not taking my son away from me on Thanksgiving."

Her lips quirked. "So now it's suddenly a super-important family holiday?"

Staring at her full, wet lips, he murmured, "It's growing on me." Then he looked up. "Tess and Stefano? You don't mean Prince Stefano Zacco, the fashion billionaire?"

"That's him."

"You're best friends with Zacco's wife?" His eyes narrowed. "And what about the other one… Hallie? Do I know her?"

Lola gave him a cheeky grin. "You often stay at her husband's hotels."

His eyes widened. "She's married to Cristiano Moretti? Your best friends are both married to billionaires?"

"So?"

"Were they the ones who were going to help you fight for custody?"

She nodded. "We look out for each other."

So she'd never been plotting with Sergei Morozov behind his back. All his irrational fears had been just that—*irrational*. As she set down her phone, he said quietly, "I'm sorry I doubted you."

"Yeah. You should stop it." Putting a hand on her hip, she gave him a tilted glance beneath her dark lashes. "Get this through your head. I'll never betray you, Rodrigo. Ever."

Hearing Lola speak those words caused a strange rush through his heart. His gaze fell to her full, lush breasts in the bra, traveling down her nearly naked body, to her tiny bare waist, expanding to the curve of her hips, with the little flimsy black lace panties. Behind her in the mirror, he could see most of her backside, with only the tiny strip between.

"Show me," he whispered.

Pulling her into his arms, he lowered his mouth to hers. Pushing her against the wall of the changing room, he gloried in the feel of the soft curves of her body pressed against his own. He felt the tremble of her lips. Felt her hesitate.

He lured her, tempted her. He gripped her wrists to the wall, ruthlessly kissing her until her lips began to move against his, slowly at first, then hungrily, as her fire matched his own.

Pulling her wrists from his grip, she wrapped her arms around his shoulders, drawing him down harder against her.

Outside their small changing room, in the exclusive, private waiting area, their baby was still noisily snoring in the stroller, parked beside the white leather sofa and three-way mirror. For now, they were alone, but at any moment, Rodrigo knew they could be interrupted. Perhaps the boutique's salesgirls would come in to offer him more champagne, or bring more ball gowns for his wife to try on. He glanced back at the waiting area. For all he knew, there were security cameras.

He should take her back to his apartment, he knew, where they could be assured of privacy. But it would take too long. It would be twenty minutes. Thirty.

He needed her *now*.

Jerking the velvet curtain closed over the changing room doorway, Rodrigo kissed her passionately, cradling her face in his hands.

She was so sweet. So indescribably sweet. His earlier suspicions had melted away, and his heart was full of an emotion he didn't want to identify.

I'll never betray you, Rodrigo. Ever.

Lola belonged to him, him alone, now and forever.

Her long blond hair tumbled down her back as he slowly kissed down her throat. Her skin smelled of vanilla and summer, soft, warm and sweet. He felt her tremble as he caressed her bare arms, to her naked waist, his hands running over the hot skin of her back. He unhooked her bra, letting it drop to the parquet floor.

He cupped her full, magnificent breasts, and heard her intake of breath. Lowering his head, he kissed her creamy skin, all the while running his hands over her hips, her back, her delectable backside.

He was hard. Aching. It felt like he'd been hard for days, wanting her. It was some kind of strange magic: no matter how many times he possessed her, he hungered for more.

Her initial hesitation had disappeared, replaced by fierce, undisguised desire. It was something he'd always loved about Lola. She never tried to hide her desire for him, which only made him want her more, making the fire inside him burn hotter still. Holding her in his arms, in this small enclosed space, he felt a sense of urgency, knowing they could be discovered at any moment.

He stroked the edge of her black lace panties, letting his fingertips trail over her skin, from her hip around the curve of her leg to her thighs. He lightly grazed his hand over the lace, then moved the fabric aside to slowly stroke her beneath it.

She was wet. Hot and wet. He felt her tremble, heard her sharp intake of breath, and he wanted more. He wanted to hear her gasp and feel her shake as she shattered beneath his touch.

Kneeling, he peeled off the panties. Lifting her leg over his shoulder, he paused between her legs. For a moment, he inhaled the scent of her, letting her feel the warmth of his breath, teasing her. And when he felt her shiver, he pressed his mouth against her skin and tasted her.

She gasped, one of her hands pressing against the wall, the other gripping his shoulder with increasing intensity as he worked her with his tongue, one moment swirling the taut wet nub, then lapping her with the full width of his tongue.

She gave a sudden muffled cry, biting her lip to choke back the noise. But he felt the full force of her explosion by her fingernails gripping into his skin, deep enough to draw blood.

He'd given her pleasure, but it wasn't enough. He wanted to give her more. Much more.

His wife was naked, but he was still fully clothed.

Rising unsteadily to his feet, he unzipped his fly. Lifting her against the wall, he wrapped her naked legs around his hips. In a single thrust, he buried his shaft, thick and hard, deep inside her.

So sweet. So hot. So tight. Holding her backside with the width of his hands, he felt a wave of pleasure as he filled her. He groaned in ecstasy.

She gasped, her hips moving against him, her legs tightening around him as he pushed inside her, riding her against the wall. Then he made the mistake of looking at her face.

Lola's eyes were shut, her beautiful face glowing with sensual, almost sacred joy.

Seeing that, he lost control. With a low growl, he thrust deep inside her, hard and fast. This time, she screamed with pleasure, uncaring of who might hear them. And at that, he exploded, spilling himself inside her with a low, ragged roar.

They barely had a moment to catch their breath, when, in the private waiting room beyond the velvet curtain, they heard a surprised snuffle, followed by a plaintive wail.

"Now you did it." With her legs still wrapped around his hips, Lola gave him a heavy-lidded grin. "You woke the baby."

"I did?" He returned her grin. "You were louder."

"Your fault," she said loftily.

For a moment, they just smiled at each other tenderly, their bodies still entwined. He felt that strange burst of happiness, coming from the vicinity of his heart.

His heart.

A chill went through him. Abruptly, he released her, letting her feet slide to the floor. Not looking at her, he zipped up his fly.

"I'll go take care of Jett," he mumbled, and left her, closing the velvet curtain abruptly behind him.

As he took their baby out of the stroller, comforting Jett after the noise had woken him from his cozy nap, Rodrigo pulled a bottle from the bag tucked in the bottom of the stroller. He tried to tell himself he hadn't felt what he'd felt. It was good sex. That was all. Just sex.

"Everything is all right, *señor*?" An alarmed salesgirl looked in on the private waiting area. "We heard a noise. It sounded like a scream."

Rodrigo gave her his coldest, most supercilious stare. "My son woke up from his nap. Surely that's not a problem. If it is, we can shop elsewhere."

"No, no, of course not, *señor*." The salesgirl backed away. "Let us know if your lovely wife needs anything more."

He stared after her.

His lovely wife already had everything she needed. His fortune. His name. His body. She needed no more.

She'd loved him once. She wouldn't make that mistake again.

And neither would he. Every time he'd loved a woman, she betrayed him. Was every woman faithless? Or was there something about Rodrigo that made them so, from the moment he loved them?

He didn't know, but it had happened not just once, not twice, but three times. He wouldn't make it four.

These feelings he felt for Lola were sexual, nothing more. And that was all they could ever be.

CHAPTER SEVEN

THE NEXT NIGHT, as they walked into the large, elegant ball-room of a grand hotel on the Gran Vía, Lola kept sneaking glances at her husband on her arm.

Over the last twenty-four hours, they'd made love six times. Before she'd even stopped blushing from the shocking sexual encounter in the luxury clothing boutique they'd barely gotten home when Rodrigo had started kissing her again. In the great room with its view of the autumn colors of Retiro Park, Rodrigo had pulled her onto the sofa, and made love to her, this time taking off his own clothes, with gentle, seductive urgency.

Later that night, once their baby was properly asleep in his crib and they had hours to call their own, Rodrigo had made love to her again, slowly, lingeringly caressing every inch of her. As if they had the rest of their lives to enjoy each other.

Which they did.

Lola didn't understand how any woman could ever be unfaithful to Rodrigo. And she wasn't the only one, apparently. Even his ex that she'd spoken with on set yesterday, the famous actress Pia Ramirez, had seemed bewildered by it.

"So you're Rodrigo's new wife," the older actress had said. "I'd started to think he would never marry."

"And you're the one who cheated on him," Lola had

replied bluntly. The other woman's eyebrows raised, as if she were trying to decide whether to be offended; then she'd sighed.

"I loved Rodrigo, with the impetuous love of the young. He was working, chasing his empire. While he was gone—" she'd lifted her hands helplessly "—a handsome actor started paying attention to me every day. He said he was desperately in love, that he would die for me. But after he got me into bed, somehow, pictures were sent of us to Rodrigo." She'd looked away. "I'm happy now, married with a family. But I still wonder sometimes who sent those photos. And who that man was. I never saw him again. But he destroyed everything."

"You destroyed it," Lola said coldly. Then her phone buzzed, and she'd been distracted by funny messages from Tess and Hallie in New York, begging her to come for Thanksgiving.

But the more Lola thought about it, the more confused she was by the whole thing. She looked up at him now, in the gilded ballroom of the grand nineteenth-century hotel. How could anyone betray Rodrigo?

He looked impossibly attractive, dressed in a sleek tuxedo that accentuated the hard, powerful shape of his muscular body. Even now, while he was surrounded by people congratulating him on getting his award, his dark eyes lingered on Lola in the slinky, low-cut red dress she'd chosen from the boutique.

He'd helped her put it on tonight in their bedroom. Then, after taking one look at her, he'd helped her swiftly take it off again. Which is why they'd arrived twenty minutes late. Her cheeks went hot, remembering.

It wasn't like her to blush. But her husband did that to her. He peeled away her defenses, leaving her trembling and gasping and hot. Just as he'd peeled away her lingerie in that shop.

As they walked through the crowded ballroom, as they ate dinner at the head table, as she saw her husband honored by his peers, Lola basked in the glory of being his wife. Especially since he made it clear to everyone that it wasn't just his glory, but hers. Whenever anyone congratulated Rodrigo, he said: "It was entirely my wife's idea. She should be getting this award with me." His dark, sensual gaze simmered through hers. "I'll thank you later, believe me."

She shivered. She didn't think she'd ever get enough of him *thanking* her.

Her heart was bursting with pride as she watched him go up to the podium, to thunderous applause. But as he started his speech on stage, someone plopped beside her at the table in the darkened audience, into his empty chair.

Looking in surprise, she saw Ulrika Lund, the well-known director, whom Rodrigo had briefly been engaged to after Pia Ramirez, some eight years before.

"So you're the wife," Ulrika said without preamble. She was very thin, with muscular arms, and dressed in severe black.

"Do you mind?" Lola said, annoyed. "I'm trying to hear his speech."

"I'm sure you are, because he's praising you. He praised me once, too. For about a day." Her jaw tightened. "But as soon as I agreed to marry him, he was suddenly too busy to see me."

"Is that your excuse for cheating on him?" Lola said coldly, looking up at her handsome husband on the stage, wishing the woman would go away.

Ulrika leaned forward, drumming her fingers impatiently. "I met another man while Rodrigo was gone. A man who hung on my every word. Eventually I gave in. Then someone sent Rodrigo photographs of our night together. That gave him a convenient excuse to end our engagement." She paused. "I never saw the other man again.

Even when I tried to find him. I discovered he'd given me a fictitious name."

A warning buzz went off in the back of Lola's mind. It sounded almost exactly like the story that Pia Ramirez had told. *Coincidence*, she told herself firmly. Pushing the disquieting thought aside, she said, "And this affects me how?"

"I think Rodrigo was behind it."

"Don't be ridiculous," Lola bit out. As her husband continued to speak on stage, other people at the table looked in irritation at their whispers.

"It took me a while to figure it out," Ulrika said with a hard stare. "But every time Rodrigo gets close to a woman, he sabotages it. I used to blame myself, but not anymore. Not after it happened in all three of his engagements." She looked at Lola. "He actually married you. So the devastation will be twice as crushing when it comes."

"It won't—because I'd never cheat on him!"

"Don't get comfortable. That's what I came to tell you. Because you won't be with him for long." The woman glanced up at the stage, her lips twisting bitterly. "He'll see to that."

And she left.

Lola felt dizzy as she tried to focus back on stage. Her husband was smiling, gripping the edges of the podium, looking out of his spotlight toward the thousand film industry people sitting at tables in the ballroom.

"And most of all, I'd like to thank my former assistant, now my wife, for being the reason I'm here tonight, accepting this award. And more importantly, for giving me the greatest gift of all—our baby son."

There was a low *awwww* from the crowd, and then applause, scattered at first, then building to a roar, as he smiled for the crowd and, gripping his gold statuette high, left the stage.

But Lola only dimly heard his words or the crowd's

adoring response. All she could suddenly think about was the stranger who'd shown up in California, when Rodrigo was in South America. The stranger who'd come out of nowhere to chat with her on the beach.

Are you all alone? You're too beautiful to be lonely. Would you like some company? You and your charming baby?

He'd made her nervous, but she'd told herself it was just typical California friendliness. And as for the man's uncanny good looks, well, half of Los Angeles were out-of-work actors. Good-looking people were the norm, not the exception.

But now the whole thing had a surreal, almost sinister aspect.

Every time Rodrigo gets close to a woman, he sabotages it. I used to blame myself, but not anymore. Not after it happened in all three of his engagements.

No. Lola took a deep breath. It couldn't be true. He wouldn't sabotage his own engagements. Why would he?

She had the sudden memory of his face when they'd returned to the apartment in Madrid. He'd looked almost— haunted.

And yet she knew he'd grown up surrounded by wealth, with both parents. She'd always assumed he'd had a happy childhood, growing up in privilege. But now, not for the first time, she wondered about the dark shadows she'd seen in his eyes. Not just in Madrid, but from the day they'd met. That edge of cold ruthlessness in him, beneath his civilized veneer.

Together, you and I can give him a better childhood than we had. Either of us.

She'd never seen a picture of his parents or even of Rodrigo as a child, she suddenly realized. No family pictures, not in his beach house or anywhere else. And the story he'd told of his parents abandoning him on Thanksgiving, leaving him with the cook. Who did that?

What didn't she know about his past?

A trickle of ice went down her spine. Could Ulrika Lund's suspicions have a shred of truth?

I still wonder sometimes who sent those photos. Pia Ramirez had sounded bewildered. *And who that man was. I never saw him again. But he destroyed everything.*

Was it remotely possible that Rodrigo could have hired those men himself to try to seduce them, as a test of his fiancées' loyalty?

Or, worse, as Ulrika had suggested, because Rodrigo just wanted a good excuse to end those engagements?

No, Lola thought desperately. *Rodrigo's not like that. He wouldn't do that.*

But she knew he had a cold, ruthless streak. She thought of the way he'd cut her so abruptly out of his life because he'd seen a few lingerie photos and heard a vicious, untrue rumor.

Right after she'd dared to say she loved him.

"Well?" Rodrigo sat down beside her, putting the gold statuette on the table with a grin. "How did I do?"

"It was very good," she said, wishing she'd been able to actually listen to his speech, rather than the unsettling ideas that Ulrika had put in her head.

"I meant it." His dark eyes focused on her intently. "Every word."

"Oh. Um." She bit her lip, lowering her gaze, feeling the smiling gaze of others around them at the table. "Good."

Lola wondered what he'd say if she told him about Ulrika's accusation. Surely, Rodrigo would laugh. Yes. He'd laugh. Then they'd both laugh together.

And yet, she couldn't force the words out. Because she was scared of what would happen. Scared of what he'd say.

Lola remembered again that man on the beach. Walking

alone, without any apparent reason to be there. Or any way of getting there, unless he'd climbed over the cliffs jutting out into the ocean. Why would anyone do that?

Unless he was paid.

Unless it was his job.

How easy would it be to hire an actor willing to do underhanded work for exceptionally high pay? Especially for a billionaire who happened to own an international conglomerate of television networks and film studios?

"Lola? Did you hear me?"

She blinked up at Rodrigo, sitting beside her in the hotel's grand ballroom in the center of Madrid. "Yes, I mean, no. What did you say?"

He looked at her like she was crazy. "I've decided I'll go with you and the baby to New York for Thanksgiving."

An unexpected smile lifted her lips. "You will?"

"If nothing else, I can use the time to negotiate with Cristiano Moretti for a deal with his hotels." He grinned. "Though I know what you're thinking."

"I doubt that," she said faintly.

"You're going to tell me that I work too much. That Thanksgiving is a time for friends and family."

"Yes. Exactly." She turned away, reaching for her tiny handbag so he couldn't see her expression. "I'll let Tess know to expect us."

As she sent a message on her phone, the ballroom lights suddenly became brighter, as guests began to take their leave. With a deep breath, she looked up at her devastatingly handsome husband, sitting beside her, barely acknowledging people's congratulations as they passed by. His dark gaze was focused only on her.

"Shall we take advantage of the housekeeper watching Jett tonight, and go to the after-party?" Leaning forward to tuck hair behind her ear, he whispered huskily, "Or would you rather go home?"

Lola tried to pull away. To keep her body from responding to his touch. To be guarded and cold. To protect herself, just in case her worst fears were true.

But she couldn't.

"Home," she breathed, searching his gaze.

"Good." Her husband cupped her cheek, his dark eyes lazy as he gave her a sensual smile. Exactly, Lola thought with a shiver, like a cat would look at the mouse in its claws.

"You're sure this is it?" Lola said nervously, juggling their whining baby in her arms.

Rodrigo stopped ahead of her down the hall, pushing the empty stroller. Double-checking the number, he looked back at her.

"There are only two on the penthouse level," he said, waiting for her to catch up. "This is it."

Lola saw the number clearly on the door, and felt foolish. But then, she'd felt foolish a lot today.

After their five-day trip to Madrid, they'd left for New York later than planned yesterday. Jett had been fussy on the plane. He was teething, which made the baby irritable and unable to sleep, which made him miserable. Which made his parents miserable, too.

They'd woken up exhausted that morning in Rodrigo's luxurious SoHo loft, cranky and tired from a transatlantic flight followed by a sleepless night. Her husband had suggested they let the baby sleep in that morning, and the two of them enjoy the time in bed.

But Lola had dreamed of seeing the New York Thanksgiving Day parade since she'd watched it on television with her mother, long ago, and then later, when her mother worked on that day, with her little sisters. She was determined that their baby's first holiday season would be magical, starting with this Thanksgiving weekend in New York.

So she'd insisted on waking Jett up, getting everyone

dressed and out early into the cold, icy morning to wait on snow-covered streets. They'd watched the parade from Rodrigo's specially arranged VIP seats, and at first, it hadn't gone too badly. Holding their bundled-up baby in her lap, as they waited for the parade to begin, Lola had felt excitement that exceeded the cold nip of the air. This was exactly the life she'd yearned for when she was younger. This moment. Being a family. Having enough money to be safe and secure. Jett was having the childhood she'd only dreamed of as a girl.

Reaching for Rodrigo's gloved hand, she'd whispered, "Thank you."

He looked surprised, then his dark eyes gleamed. "All this for some seats at a parade?"

"You don't understand." She blinked hard in the cold air. "My whole childhood, I dreamed of this. The life only rich people could have. To be in New York for the Thanksgiving parade, and see real snow, and eat a pretzel on the street and spend New Year's Eve in Times Square…"

"You know that you don't have to be rich for any of that, don't you?"

"And a big expensive Christmas tree. And a mansion in Beverly Hills."

"Beverly Hills? Malibu isn't good enough?"

"I know. That part was silly." She looked down. "But my first Christmas in LA, when I was still trying to be an actress, I delivered flowers for a shop in Beverly Hills. I saw all these gorgeous mansions decorated for Christmas, and sometimes I'd see the people who lived there. There was one house in particular, once owned by silent film stars. El Corazón, I think it was called. One Christmas Eve I saw the family who lived in it and I dreamed…"

"Dreamed of what?"

Catching herself, she flashed a crooked grin. "Dreamed of their mountains of presents around the tree."

"Ah." His voice was amused. "Mountains of presents in a Beverly Hills mansion. That does take money."

As he took her hand in his own, Lola wouldn't meet his eyes. Her dream hadn't been mountains of presents, but something less tangible. She'd seen just a brief flash of the wealthy, perfect family, the handsome husband playing with his children as his wife answered the door in an apron, obviously just come from baking some kind of holiday treats. All of them glowing with health, happiness and love. To Lola, heartbroken over her baby sisters, with just five dollars to her name, that life had seemed as perfect and untouchable as their magnificent manicured gardens beyond the walls.

Lifting a dark eyebrow, Rodrigo said wickedly, his fingers tightening over hers, "But you're getting ahead of yourself, *querida*. Santa brings mountains of presents only to those who are good, not naughty like you."

"Oh, but I've been good," Lola whispered, leaning toward him on the VIP bench as they waited for the parade to begin. Reaching out with her glove, she'd cupped his cheek, still dark with five o'clock shadow as they'd rushed out that morning early with no time for him to shave. "I've been very, very good. But maybe I can be even better…"

Rodrigo's black eyes had gleamed as he leaned down to kiss her.

Then their tired, irritable baby burst into a plaintive cry in Lola's arms.

She spent the next hour juggling him, with a pacifier and a teething toy. She was so frantic, bouncing him in her lap to keep him from crying, that she barely noticed the enormous balloon floats finally fly past or the marching bands pass by. As Jett continued to fuss, she imagined people around them judging her harshly for bringing a five-month-old baby to sit outside in the freezing cold morning for a parade that took hours. She glared at someone who dared to look at her. She would have yelled something rude, but Rodrigo suddenly took the baby from her.

"Relax," he told Lola firmly. Then he looked down at the baby in his lap. "Don't keep your mother from enjoying her parade, *mi pequeñito*."

The baby looked up at his father, tears still staining his plump face, his lips parted. But something about the low rumble of Rodrigo's chest seemed to calm the baby. Frowning, Jett waved a chubby arm in his father's direction, then chomped quietly on his chew toy, staring up at the big cartoon balloons in the sky.

Lola just stared at them together, tears burning behind her eyes.

After all her years of dreaming about seeing the parade in New York, she barely remembered it afterward. What she remembered was the way Rodrigo had comforted their baby.

After they left, they'd visited an expensive toy store, where Rodrigo ordered thousands of dollars of toys for Jett without once looking at a price. Since Jett wasn't fussing, it was all enjoyable. Until Lola suggested having the toys delivered to their SoHo loft.

"It'll be delivered to California," he said firmly. "That's our home."

Lola felt deflated. "I know. But it's so nice being back in New York. That's where my friends live. My sisters."

"My accountant said your sisters still haven't cashed the check you sent them for college. Did the girls ever contact you?"

"Um… No. Not yet." Her heart tightened. She was trying not to think about that, or what it might mean. She rushed to say, "Maybe they've been busy. You know how teenagers can be…"

"They might be thoughtless, but what about their parents?"

Lola thought of the one and only time she'd spoken to her sisters' adoptive parents, when she'd showed up unannounced at their suburban home seven years before. When, while the girls had clung to their new mother, their father had told Lola to get the hell out before he called the police.

Lola pushed the painful memory away. A lot had changed since then. Surely they would realize they had nothing to fear from her now, and they'd accept her gift? And, you know, send a thank-you note or something?

But they hadn't. Even that big check hadn't made them want to talk to her.

Lola's heart twisted, but she turned away with a shrug. "It doesn't matter. Eventually I'll get through to them." Biting her lip, she looked up. "Though it would be easier if we lived here in New York instead of California…"

His face shuttered. "No."

Tilting her head, Lola said thoughtfully, "Did you know that as the film industry is increasingly a worldwide market, New York has become a hotbed of media companies that will dominate the future of the entertainment business?"

Rodrigo looked as if he were fighting a smile. "You just made that up."

Her lips quirked. "It could be true."

Rodrigo snorted, shaking his head. Then, as they'd left the toy store, he'd said quietly, "I'm sorry, *querida*, but we live in California. Enjoy your time here while it lasts."

Now, as they stood in the hallway of Tess's new co-op building, Lola looked at her husband, her heart in her throat.

Enjoy your time while it lasts.

Would their marriage last? Or would that, too, soon end?

Every time Rodrigo gets close to a woman, he sabotages it… He actually married you. So the devastation will be twice as crushing when it comes.

"Well?" he said sharply, standing in front of the penthouse door. "You were so worried about getting here on time. What are you waiting for?"

"Nothing." But as Lola lifted her hand to knock, she heard people laughing inside the apartment, and hesitated.

Looking at the huge diamond ring on her left hand, she suddenly wished she'd told Tess and Hallie the news of her marriage over the phone. Earlier, she'd grinned at the thought of seeing the shock on their faces, that Lola, the one who'd bossed the other two girls into telling their ex-lovers about their babies, had suddenly—without warning—married her own baby's father.

Because, unlike her friends, Lola had always refused to reveal the identity of her baby's father. Hallie and Tess had crazy theories about who Jett's father might be—that the man was married or some kind of criminal. Tess was especially good at coming up with eye-popping theories.

She hadn't wanted to tell them the simple truth, that Jett's father was Lola's old boss. She'd been trying to forget his existence, and thought if she didn't say Rodrigo's name, she wouldn't think about him, either.

But now, she felt like she was springing the news on her friends out of nowhere. *Hey, you know how I stubbornly refused to tell you anything about Jett's father? Well, here he is! And he's a Spanish billionaire! Ha-ha! And guess what? We're married!*

Well, Lola consoled herself wryly, at least the two women wouldn't be able to complain about having yet another bridesmaid's dress gathering dust in their closets for eternity.

Squaring her shoulders, she knocked hard on the door.

A moment later, it opened, and she saw Tess's beaming, pink-cheeked face, her red hair tumbling over her shoulders.

"Lola!" she squealed. She turned to call over her shoulder, "Hallie! Lola's here!"

The brunette came quickly, almost at a run. Lola came

inside carrying Jett, Rodrigo following a moment behind her, pushing the empty stroller. Helping her and the baby off with their winter coats, he disappeared behind the closet door. Tess's eyes went wide, and she looked at Lola, her eyes full of questions.

"I like your new place, Tess," Lola said evasively, looking around the gorgeous penthouse, with two-story windows overlooking most of snowy Central Park. "But where's your furniture?"

"It hasn't arrived from Italy yet. We've only just got the keys." She glanced back at her husband, who'd come up behind her. "Stefano wanted to wait and host New Year's Eve instead—"

"But Tess insisted on Thanksgiving," the Sicilian prince said, wrapping his arms around his wife's waist, who giggled.

"I'll host New Year's Eve," Hallie's husband, Cristiano, yelled from the next room.

"Anyway." Rolling her eyes, Tess turned to Lola. "We had to have the meal catered, but I knew you and Hallie wouldn't care if we sat on folding chairs. Love is what matters, right?"

"I couldn't agree more," Stefano said, nuzzling his wife. Then he seemed to remember they were surrounded by people, and straightened. His eyes focused on Rodrigo, who'd just closed the closet door. "Cabrera? What the hell are you doing here?"

"Rodrigo Cabrera!" Tess exclaimed, clapping her hands together. "I knew I recognized you!"

"Hey, Zacco." Looking at Tess, he said politely, "Thank you for the invitation to Thanksgiving."

Tess looked utterly bewildered.

"Who's he?" Hallie demanded, her face puzzled as she stared at Rodrigo. "Why is he pushing Jett's stroller?"

Behind her, Cristiano wandered in carrying an empty

tray. "Table's all set," he said with pride, then stopped when he saw Rodrigo. "Who are you?"

Lola took a deep breath.

This was it. The moment of her big announcement. She thought she'd feel smug and cheeky. Instead, she just felt awkward.

"This is Rodrigo Cabrera," she began. "I used to work for him in California. He's…um…" She looked at him, then mumbled, "Well, he's the father of my baby."

"What?" Tess said.

"No, seriously?" Hallie said.

"That's not my only news." Adjusting her baby against her hip, Lola lifted her left hand, letting the huge diamond engagement ring glitter in the light.

Her friends gasped.

"I can't believe it," Hallie said, grabbing her hand to look closer at the ring.

"And we're not just engaged. We're…we're married."

"Married!"

"I knew it!" Tess cried, practically bouncing with joy. Reaching out, she stroked Jett's soft, downy hair. "I knew you wouldn't love someone who was no good!"

At the word *love*, Lola's cheeks went hot, and she glanced back self-consciously at Rodrigo. But he'd been drawn across the room to accept the raucous, teasing congratulations of the two other men.

"Why didn't you tell us?" Hallie said softly, her soft brown eyes accusing. "We imagined your baby's father must be a total disaster, since you refused to tell us his name." She eyed Rodrigo. "He doesn't seem so bad."

Lola looked at her husband. "He's not." Her voice trembled a little. "He's not bad at all."

The two women stared at her.

"Oh, man," Tess said. "You've got it bad."

Oh, no! The last thing Lola wanted was for that rumor

to go around, especially when Rodrigo was only ten feet away! Lola turned on the redhead with a growl.

"Don't be ridiculous. We only got married for the baby's sake. To be practical."

"So you're not having sex?" Hallie said.

Lola's cheeks went hot. "It doesn't mean anything. It's just a benefit of being married." Her voice turned husky as her eyes unwillingly returned to her handsome husband. "He's my baby's father, and I respect him, and like him so much…"

Hallie followed her gaze, then the usually sensible brunette said, almost in awe, "Tess is right. You love him like crazy." She slowly looked over Lola's black cashmere sweater and leggings and knee-high boots. "It's written all over you."

"Hush!" Lola angrily grabbed Hallie's arm. "He'll hear you."

The brunette looked bewildered. "And that would be a bad thing?"

"Yes," said Tess, looking at Lola's face. Taking Jett from her arms, the redhead waved for them to follow. "Come in here." Turning toward the men, she said loudly, "We'll be in the kitchen."

Prince Stefano called, "Need help?"

"No, we, um, Lola wants a good recipe for pie and she was wondering whether to use butter or shortening for crust."

"Oh," said Stefano, his eyes glazing over.

"Let's go watch the game," Cristiano said heartily. "My father's already in there, keeping an eye on Esme and Jack. You coming, Cabrera?"

"What game?" Rodrigo said.

The other two men laughed. "It's Thanksgiving, isn't it? The Cowboys. Come on."

"Men and sports," Hallie sighed with a fond smile, shaking her head as the men disappeared.

"This way." Still holding Lola's baby, Tess led them down the hall to a gorgeous kitchen which looked completely untouched.

"We're still waiting for our pots and pans," she said apologetically. "Stefano offered to buy everything new and have it delivered yesterday, but I just want our old things from Sicily. I didn't think you'd mind eating off the caterer's plates." She bit her lip, suddenly looking worried. "You don't mind, do you? Is it tacky?"

"Not at all," Hallie said soothingly.

Looking around, Lola said in sudden worry, "But we're having a real dinner, right?" She added apologetically, "It's just that it's Rodrigo's first real Thanksgiving—"

"Don't worry." Tess's round face broke into a big smile. "Dinner's being catered from one of the best restaurants in the city. Well, except for the rolls and pies. Those are being brought by my cousins. Did you hear? They're running the family bakery now."

"Your cousins!" Lola was astounded. "But they're so young!"

"Just a few years younger than we are. Old enough to know what they want in life." Tess's smile lifted to a grin. "But obviously still learning the business. They called to say they're running a little late."

"But I'm sure Tess didn't really drag us into the kitchen to talk about pie." Hallie leaned back against the spotless marble counter, her dark eyes piercing. "What's going on with you and your new husband, Lola?"

"And how could you have a wedding without us?" Tess looked suddenly hurt. "We should have been bridesmaids. Just like you were for us."

Lola's first instinct was to refuse to explain, to make an excuse, to grab her babbling baby out of Tess's arms and wander into the front room to join the men watching football.

But suddenly, her heart was in her throat. Tears lifted to her eyes.

"Lola?" Hallie said.

"Lola, are you all right?" Tess said.

Her friends looked shocked. They had never seen her vulnerable before. Lola had always prided herself on being the strong one. She was the bossy one giving them advice, not the other way around.

"I'm sorry," Lola whispered, wiping her eyes. "I didn't sleep well last night."

"Do you want a cupcake?" asked Tess anxiously.

"A glass of wine?" asked Hallie.

It was so typical, Lola unwillingly laughed through her tears.

Then, with an intake of breath, she told them everything.

Her poverty and helplessness as a child, seeing her mother work herself to death, seeing her stepfather injured, disabled and finally sent to prison for trying to sell drugs. How Lola had felt, being responsible for her baby sisters when she was still a child herself. How, after their mother's untimely death, the girls had been dragged away from her, their screams still ringing in her ears. How she'd felt at eighteen, seeing them happy in another family, having forgotten her completely.

"I decided that money was the only thing that mattered," she whispered. She looked down. "I did some things I'm not proud of."

Hallie patted her shoulder. "We all have. It's part of being human."

"Oh, Lola." Tess looked heartbroken. "I never imagined. You always seemed so tough."

"Like nothing could hurt you," said Hallie.

Lola choked out a laugh, then wiped her eyes. "I pushed you guys so hard, while I was a coward in my own life."

"No, never," Tess said loyally.

"You helped us," Hallie said.

"So now let us help you," the redhead said. "Do you love him?"

"No, I—" But Lola's words caught in her throat. Memories flooded through her of Rodrigo tenderly taking care of their baby. Of him caring for her. Of all their days talking, and the hot nights when he'd made love to her again and again. Looking at her friends, she couldn't lie to them.

With a shuddering breath, she whispered, "I don't know."

Hallie and Tess looked at each other.

"You don't know?" Hallie said gently.

"I can't love him." Lola wiped her eyes. "I did once, last year, before I knew I was pregnant. But when I told him my feelings, he found an excuse to break up with me, and practically tossed me out of California. He doesn't believe in love. He thinks it only brings pain." She hesitated, then said quietly, "He was engaged three times before he met me."

Idealistic Tess looked shocked. *"Three times?"*

"And they all cheated on him before the wedding."

"All of them?" Hallie said faintly.

"I'm sorry I didn't invite you to the wedding. But as soon as Rodrigo found out about the baby, he insisted we get married at once. A judge was waiting at his loft to marry us right after the paternity test. With his housekeeper and bodyguard as witnesses."

"You didn't even get to plan your own wedding?" Tess said indignantly.

Lola looked down.

"It wasn't so bad," she said in a small voice.

"And whoever heard of a man engaged so many times?" Hallie said wonderingly.

"It happens," Lola said, a hard edge coming into her voice. She felt suddenly protective of him.

Tess's plump face was bewildered. "And all three women cheated on him before the wedding?"

Lola took a deep breath, wondering if she should tell them the worst, the fear she could barely even admit to herself—that he'd arranged those betrayals himself, either to test their loyalty or have an excuse to end the relationships.

He's not like that, Lola told herself desperately. *He wouldn't do something so underhanded.*

The house phone rang on the kitchen counter. Tess picked it up. "Hello?" Her face lit up. "Yes, of course. Send them all up!" Hanging up, she said happily, "That was the doorman. My cousins are here, and so are the caterers!" Moving to the wide, open doorway, she called, "Boys! The food's here!"

There was a loud yell of glee, and the trampling of heavy male feet.

"Will you be all right, Lola?"

Hallie's voice was quiet behind her. Lola turned to see the brunette's worried eyes.

With a deep breath, she lifted her chin. "Don't worry about me. I'm just being silly." Wiping the last of the tears from her eyes, she took Jett back into her arms with a smile. "Rodrigo and I are happy. We have a baby together. We're married. Friends." She gave a crooked smile. "And the sex is fantastic."

Gentle, romantic Tess looked at her. "But without love, how can it last?"

Don't get comfortable, Ulrika Lund had said. *You won't be with him for long. He'll see to that.*

As Lola looked between the worried faces of her best friends, a trickle of fear went down her spine.

I have to understand what happened, she thought suddenly. Had her husband really been behind all those betrayals and broken engagements? Or was it just a wild coincidence?

She'd spoken to his first two fiancées, but not the third, Elise Patel, a world-famous composer who now lived in Los Angeles. Perhaps her story would turn out to be completely different.

Lola's eyes narrowed. One way or the other, she would find out the truth.

CHAPTER EIGHT

IT WAS STRANGE, Rodrigo thought, to have one's first Thanksgiving at the age of thirty-seven. But no stranger than the rest of it, he supposed.

He looked down the long table, surrounded by mismatched folding chairs, in this magnificent, half-empty Manhattan penthouse overlooking Central Park. It was strange to be eating a traditional Thanksgiving dinner off the caterer's rented china, surrounded mostly by strangers.

Rodrigo knew Prince Stefano Zacco, the luxury fashion mogul, only slightly. His only acquaintance with Cristiano Moretti was that he'd often stayed in the man's hotels.

Rodrigo had no memory whatsoever of when Stefano's wife, Tess, had apparently worked as a waitress at one of his cocktail parties. He'd never met Hallie before, nor Cristiano's father who'd just come from Italy, nor Tess's two young cousins, who looked barely old enough to be out of high school, but who apparently now ran the family bakery and, he had to admit, certainly knew how to bake.

This Thanksgiving was strange, for sure.

But in some ways, it wasn't strange at all. It was exactly how Rodrigo had imagined it might be, when he was a child left on his own in Madrid to eat *arroz con pollo* with the nanny and the cook, as his mother flew off to ski in Aspen with her latest lover, and his cold, distant father disappeared to quietly rage at a film set.

Now, as Rodrigo sat at the table, listening to all of the people around him laugh and joke and tease each other, he felt like he was on a film set himself. A scene for a Thanksgiving movie, or an advertisement for any holiday that brought family and friends together for a meal. He ate the butter-basted turkey and cornbread stuffing, the mashed potatoes and gravy and fresh cranberry sauce, and it was all so delicious. After eating a huge plateful of food, he'd gone back for a second—having been told it was tradition to eat until one was utterly stuffed—and afterward, he found himself relaxing into warmth and pleasure, smiling as Lola and her friends good-naturedly fought over who got the wishbone.

"It's mine," Lola said ferociously, holding one side of the wishbone.

"No way, mine," Hallie retorted, gripping the other.

"Let Lola have it," Tess whispered to Hallie. "She needs it."

The brunette instantly released it. "You win."

Rodrigo looked between them in confusion. "Why does Lola need it?"

His wife flashed him a look he couldn't read. Fear? Regret? Hope? But before he could analyze it, it was gone. She shrugged. "It's good luck, that's all."

"But why do you need luck more than anyone else?" he persisted.

She gave him a crooked smile. "I'm married to you, aren't I?"

"And I'm married to you," he pointed out, returning her grin.

"So maybe you're the one who needs it, then." She held out the wishbone. "We're supposed to wait until it dries, but I'm not that patient. Grab a side, make a wish and pull."

As ordered, he grabbed the other side of the wishbone

and pulled it, hard and fast, at the same time she did. There was a loud crack.

Rodrigo lifted his bigger piece of the wishbone. "What does this mean?"

Lola looked disconsolately at her smaller piece, then sighed. "It means you win." She gave him a strange look. "What did you wish for?"

"I didn't wish for anything," he said honestly. He looked around them. "I have everything any man could want."

Applause and approval went around the table. But he again saw that flash of emotion cross his wife's face. An emotion that he didn't understand. Emotion that was quickly veiled as she turned away. "It's time for dessert."

She was hiding something.

The insidious thought went through him like a hissing snake, twisting and curling from the base of his skull down the length of his spine.

His wife had a secret. Something she didn't want him to know.

What?

Lola, Tess and Hallie returned from the kitchen with six pies—two each of pumpkin, pecan and apple. With a flourish, Lola cut him a slice of each kind, covered them with whipped cream and slid the plate in front of him.

"Three slices?" he said, bemused.

"Try them all, then decide which one you like best." Kissing his temple, she said, "I want your first Thanksgiving to be perfect."

Rodrigo lifted his fork, to do as commanded. But as he tasted each slice of pie, all the buttery, sweet, creamy, crunchy goodness he'd anticipated tasted like ash in his mouth. As he looked at her veiled eyes, a panicked, animal suspicion skittered down his spine.

What was she hiding?

Against his will, he was flooded by memories of those

other women who'd hidden secrets. Secrets that inevitably ended with Rodrigo looking at pictures of them naked in bed with other men.

He still wondered who'd sent the photographs. One of his rivals? One of his friends? Whoever it was, they'd hovered in the shadows for a decade, looking out for him. He was grateful to them.

But he also hated them.

"So which one do you like best?" said one of Tess's cousins anxiously.

"Yes, which?" said the other.

Standing beside him at the table, Lola looked down at Rodrigo with inscrutable hazel eyes.

There was no question which woman he liked best.

His wife.

He could not bear to lose Lola. Not at any price. They were married now. A family—

Stop, Rodrigo told himself angrily. He was no longer a weak boy, lonely and desperate to be loved. He'd realized the truth long ago. Anyone he loved, he lost. That was the reality, or at least his reality.

But he didn't love Lola. Therefore, he told himself firmly, he had nothing to worry about. His investigator had already assured him she wasn't in contact with Sergei Morozov, or any other man. And having a home and financial security for Jett meant too much to her. She'd never cheat, not when it would leave her without a penny.

His shoulders slowly relaxed.

"Well?" Lola said softly, "What is your answer?"

"Kiss me," he said huskily, "and I'll tell you my favorite."

Putting her hand gently on his cheek, Lola lowered her head to his, and softly kissed him, in front of everyone. Her lips were tender and burned through his body. Through his soul. Finally, she pulled away.

"Pecan," he said, because it was closest.

"I knew it." One of Tess's cousins looked at the other triumphantly. "I told you it was the best, Natalie."

But Rodrigo wasn't thinking about pie. He looked up at his wife.

No other woman had ever been so important to him before. His life had become better from the moment Lola had come into it. He had the sudden disquieting thought that she could destroy that happiness, if she chose.

No, he told himself fiercely. *She doesn't own me. As long as I don't love her, I can trust her.*

But he saw the evasion of Lola's gaze, the wistfulness of her smile. And all the warmth and happiness of the day melted away.

Rodrigo suddenly knew one thing. He had to find out her secret. Before it was too late.

Before he got another anonymous photograph in the mail.

"Thank you for meeting me, Ms. Patel." In California a few weeks later, Lola rose from the table in the outdoor patio of the beach café, holding out her hand. "It's an honor."

"The honor is mine," said the other woman, shaking her hand. Lifting her designer sunglasses to her black, shiny hair, Elise Patel looked around them, blinking in the bright sunshine. "Honestly, it's the first time I've left my studio in weeks."

"Composing a new score?"

"Not just composing. Producing, too." Dropping her expensive designer handbag carelessly to the rough wood patio floor, she got the waiter's attention with a snap. "Triple espresso, please."

"Triple?" Tucking Jett's blanket around him in the nearby stroller, Lola said with a laugh, "If I drank that, I'd be awake for weeks."

She snorted. "I wish. I'm still trying to wake up, after three hours' sleep. I only have ten minutes before I need to get back to work." With a slight smile, she shook her head. "Honestly, I do not have time for this."

The famous composer did indeed look a little tired, with dark circles beneath her eyes, wearing oversized jeans and a plain black sweatshirt, though she'd driven up in a two-hundred-thousand-dollar SUV.

Lola leaned back in her chair. "So why did you agree to meet me?"

Elise Patel's lips curved at the edges. "I was curious to meet the woman who actually managed to marry Rodrigo Cabrera."

All around them, beautiful people were chatting, sipping their lattes at this trendy beachside café not too far from Malibu. The sun was bright in the California sky, and though it was now mid-December, the air was warm enough that, in the stroller, Jett was wearing just a T-shirt and shorts over his fat baby legs, and Lola wore a simple cotton sundress and sandals, her long blond hair in a ponytail.

"I wanted to meet you too," Lola said, sipping her cappuccino. "I've already met the other two women who cheated on him, but not you."

The composer's eyes flashed in irritation, then she gave a grudging smile. "You're direct. I like that. Saves time." She looked up at the waiter who'd arrived with her espresso. "Thank you." Taking a sip, she sat back, then sighed with pleasure. "Delicious." Elise lifted a dark eyebrow. "So did you just invite me here to insult me, or were you curious about me as well?"

"Curious about one thing." Lola leaned forward. "Why did you do it?"

"Why what? Why did I cheat on him?" The other woman rolled her eyes. "That's a rude question. There's no reason for me to answer it. Unless you're afraid you might do the same?"

"Of course not!" Lola said.

"It all seems so long ago."

"Not even five years." She knew Rodrigo had ended his engagement to Elise a year before Lola started working for him.

"Yes, five years. An eternity." Blowing the steam off her espresso, the composer shook her head good-naturedly. "Do you know how many film scores I've written since then? How many awards I've won?"

"Yes, I know you're very busy and very famous," Lola said. "Is that why you cheated on Rodrigo? For the attention?"

"I loved him, I think. But I never saw him." She took another sip of espresso. "After he proposed to me, he suddenly got very busy with work and disappeared for months. Then a gorgeous production assistant suddenly was bringing me flowers. Asking me about my work. Singing my praises. Offering me foot rubs." She shrugged. "It happened. It's not something I'm proud of."

"And you ended up falling in love with the other man?"

"Love? It was just one night." She snorted. "And the sex wasn't even good. I regretted it instantly. I might have tried to work it out with Rodrigo, but someone sent him photographs. It was all very strange. If it was meant to be a blackmail attempt, the man never asked for money. He just disappeared."

"Disappeared..." Prickles lifted on the back of Lola's neck. She looked down at Jett, burbling happily in his stroller. The story was too much a duplicate of the other women's to be a coincidence.

"Honestly, looking back I'm almost relieved it happened," the composer said. "Since he dumped me, I've devoted myself to work, and it's all paid off. Tell Rodrigo that when you see him. Tell him thanks."

"Um…all right," she said, a little surprised.

Tilting her head, Elise murmured, "I think I can see why he married you."

Lola was flattered in spite of herself. "What do you mean?"

"I heard you were his assistant. You quit your job for him. So you have nothing else going on. You can just follow him around. You're his trophy. His pet." Her lips creased. "I think that's what he actually wanted in a woman all along. So maybe your marriage will survive." She finished the espresso at a gulp, then tossed a twenty-dollar bill on the table. "Thanks for the coffee."

And the other woman left, getting into her expensive SUV and driving fast down the coastal highway.

Lola stared after her in shock.

You quit your job for him. So you have nothing else going on. You can just follow him around. You're his trophy. His pet. I think that's what he actually wanted in a woman all along. So maybe your marriage will survive.

She tapped her fingertips angrily on the table. His trophy, was she? His pet? As she signaled for the bill, her heart thrummed with anger. Lola was his wife! The mother of a tiny infant! She had *plenty* going on!

But the insult burned through her.

For most of her life, Lola had prided herself on working longer and harder than anyone else. Just as her mother once had. Being an assistant to a powerful tycoon was long, difficult work, and she'd done well. She'd thrived. And being the logistics and operations manager of their household was no joke. She—

A man walking through the restaurant patio paused as he went past her table. "Oh. Hello again."

Still lost in her indignant thoughts, Lola looked up.

For a moment, she struggled to recognize him. Tall and blond, wearing a tight T-shirt and board shorts over his muscled body, he was handsome, tanned with a white, gleaming smile.

A chill went down her spine.

"Don't you remember me?" the man said, drawing closer to her table. His eyes seemed to caress her, and so did his smile. "We met by chance a few weeks ago? On the beach?"

Lola rose up, trembling.

"Who sent you?" Her voice hardened. "Who hired you?"

The young man went pale beneath his tan. "What? Nobody!"

"Tell me!" she demanded, pounding the table.

"You're crazy," he said, backing away nervously. He looked around the patio with its view of the ocean across the street. "She's crazy!"

Turning, he practically ran from the café.

"Don't ever harass me again!" Lola yelled after him.

After the man was gone, it took some moments for her to calm down. Blood pounded through her body, making her shake. Ignoring all the open stares, she knelt before the stroller to comfort the baby, who'd started to cry. Trying to comfort herself.

"Is everything all right, Mrs. Cabrera? What did that man do?"

Looking up, she saw one of their bodyguards, whom she'd purposefully left behind at the beach house today. And not even her favorite one, Tobias. "What are you doing here, Lester?"

"Boss told me to keep an eye on you."

"To spy on me?"

The man looked uncomfortable. "He just wanted—"

"I don't care what he wanted," she snapped. "Stop following me." Tossing money on the table for her cappuccino and croissant, she tucked her bag into the stroller and stomped away from the bodyguard, to her husband's Mercedes SUV parked behind the café.

She felt sick.

Could Rodrigo have hired the handsome stranger, who looked like a cross between a surfer and out-of-work soap opera actor, to try to seduce her?

Was that why Lester was there—to follow and get pictures?

No, she told herself fiercely. But her hands shook as she buckled her baby into the SUV and tossed the stroller into the back. Taking calming breaths, she reminded herself that Rodrigo was in San Francisco on business today. He couldn't know Lola would be at this café with his ex.

The thought reassured her as she started the engine. Then she stopped, staring out at the blue ocean.

Elise Patel's phone number was unlisted. Lola had gotten it from Marnie yesterday. Rodrigo could have easily found out where she planned to be. He could have sent the stranger, either as some kind of loyalty test, or something more malicious.

Was it possible that Rodrigo was trying to get rid of her, just like the rest? Trying to end this marriage as cheaply and easily as he could, by luring her into an affair—or even just the appearance of one?

Fear went through her, followed by rage. She gripped the steering wheel.

Enough of this. She would ask him directly when he got home tonight.

No. She couldn't. If Rodrigo was innocent, if this was all just a wild coincidence, he would think she was crazy, for getting so upset over two chance encounters with a man who had been, after all, merely friendly.

After she got back to the beach house, she spent hours pacing back and forth, unable to decide. She felt like she was losing her mind.

The truth seemed to be screaming in her face.

But she didn't want it to be true. She wanted to be blind, to take whatever comfort she could, for as long as she could, while denying the evidence that was piling up all around her.

"Mrs. Cabrera?" The housekeeper looked in on her.

"What?" Lola snapped, turning on her mid-pace. At the other woman's expression, she instantly felt bad. "I'm sorry, Mrs. Lee. Did you need something?"

"You received a letter. I'll just leave it here." Leaving an envelope on the gleaming wood sideboard, the house-keeper backed away.

"A letter?" Frowning, Lola came forward. Then she saw the return address. A suburban town in New York.

Her sisters.

Heart pounding, she ripped it open.

The money she'd sent for her sisters' college fund, the six-figure check she'd sent them as an olive branch, floated gently to the floor.

They'd returned it. Uncashed.

Lola's heart lifted to her throat, choking her. Her sisters weren't interested in forgiving her. They still hated her…

But there was a note. Desperately, she clutched at it. The childish uneven handwriting looped in pencil.

Dear Lola,
Thank you for sending us this college money. Our parents said we can't accept it. We have enough and we don't need charity.
But they said we should invite you for Christmas. And I think that's a good idea because we could use a big sister. Not me, cause I have one, but Kelsey could. I'm sick of her always bragging about her memories of you and I'd like some, too.

*I'm sorry I was scared last time. I'm not scared
anymore. Please say you'll come.
Yours truly,
Johanna Sandford*

Tears rushed to Lola's eyes as she crushed the note to her
chest. A torrent of conflicting emotions rushed through her.

The last day Lola saw Johanna, she was just six, riding
her bike happily with her older sister on the shaded street
in front of their two-story white house with green shutters.
When Lola had told the girls she was going to take them
away, she'd expected them to cry with joy. Instead, they'd
clung to their mother and the family's golden retriever. Johanna's face had been terrified. After that, Lola had never
been able to face either of her sisters again.

Now, pain lifted in Lola's throat, sharp as a razor blade.
She blinked fast, looking out through the beach house's
windows. Jett was sleeping in the nursery. The room was
shadowy and silent. In the distance, she could see the pink
and orange sunset over the black ocean.

All these years, she'd been too scared to face them. She'd
told herself that they'd either forgotten her, or hated her.

Only the money—and Rodrigo—had given her the courage to finally contact them, hoping they could forgive her,
and let her back in their lives.

But they'd sent back the money. They didn't want it.

They just wanted her to come for Christmas.

She closed her eyes, holding her baby sister's note like
it was a precious gift. Raw emotions were pouring through
her like torrential rain.

*I'm sorry I was scared last time. I'm not scared
anymore.*

Then she opened her eyes, as everything became suddenly very clear.

Later that night, when Rodrigo came home from his trip, she turned on the light where she'd been sitting on the sofa, waiting for him.

"Lola." He looked surprised. "I thought you'd be asleep. What are you doing, sitting in the dark?"

Gripping her hands at her sides, she rose to her feet. "We need to talk."

Rodrigo's black eyes gleamed. "I'm glad you're awake. I've missed you, *querida*." He gave her a sensual smile. "I can hardly wait to—"

"A handsome stranger flirted with me today."

He froze, staring at her. "What?"

She shrugged. "He was just being friendly. It would be no big deal, except it's the second time he's tried. And—" she paused "—it's exactly the same thing that happened to all your other fiancées."

His expression changed. "I heard how you spent the morning. Having coffee with Elise Patel."

"Did Marnie tell you that?"

"She mentioned in passing you asked for Elise's phone number. What I don't understand is why."

"Ulrika Lund came up to me at the awards ceremony in Madrid, while you were giving your speech." Lola met his eyes evenly. "She had an interesting theory about why all your engagements ended."

"Because they were unfaithful," he said flatly.

"Yes, but why?"

He stiffened. "What kind of question is that?"

"Did you hire men to deliberately seduce them?"

Rodrigo dropped his suitcase with a loud bang against the floor. He gave a harsh laugh. "Is that some kind of joke?"

"Maybe you were just testing their loyalty. Or maybe…"

Speaking her deepest fear, she whispered, "Maybe you were afraid of loving them, and wanted to get rid of them before they got too close."

His black eyes glinted sparks in the small halo of lamp-light as he came forward. "You're insane."

Lola set her jaw, trying desperately to appear strong, but her voice wobbled as she said, "Did you send that man to flirt with me today? Are you trying to get rid of me?"

"How can you even think such a thing?" he said in a low, dangerous voice, looking down at her. "After I decide to trust you—"

"*Trust* me! Is that what you call it, when you have Lester follow me?"

"That was for your own protection!"

"No!" she cried. Her chest rose and fell in quick, angry breaths. "It was for yours!"

The two of them glared at each other with matching ferocity.

Behind him, she could see the sweep of silver moonlight through the windows. He towered over her, powerful and fierce in the shadowy great room.

Reaching out, Rodrigo gripped her shoulders, searching her gaze. "Tell me this is a joke. You know I would not do such a despicable thing."

"Tell me why, every time anyone gets close to you and starts to care, you push them away."

"If you know about my exes, you know my reason—"

"No," she said steadily. "It started before that. Because every time you got engaged, you disappeared. For weeks or months. And you did the same thing after you married me."

His expression changed. Releasing her, he turned away. Going to the wet bar, he poured himself a short glass of forty-year-old Scotch. He took a drink, then finally turned to face her. "You're right. I learned not to trust anyone long ago. When I was a boy."

"Your parents," she whispered, looking at him.

Rodrigo took another gulp of Scotch. The moonlight caressed the hard edges of his face. "My father wasn't my father."

"What?" She gasped.

"My whole childhood, I always felt like my father despised me. He never hugged me. He barely looked at me." He looked away. "At his funeral, my mother told me why. He'd known all along I wasn't his son." A sardonic smile traced his sensual lips. "She'd had a brief affair with the chauffeur. Just one of many. She enjoyed throwing his love for her back in his face."

"So that's why you wanted the paternity test," Lola said slowly. "And why you insisted on marrying me."

"I didn't want my child to ever feel like I felt that day," he said in a low voice. "Or any other days."

Lola no longer wondered why he had trust issues. Indeed, now she could only wonder that he was able to trust anyone at all.

Rodrigo stared out the window bleakly, toward the dark, moonlit beach. "Growing up, I could hardly wait to get married. I wanted a real family, a real home. But it was never real." He gave her a crooked smile. "With Pia, I fell in love with the role she played in a movie, not her. Ulrika and I just argued all the time. Elise—well, we both loved our careers more than each other."

"She said to tell you thanks, by the way. For breaking up with her. Giving her more time to work."

"That sounds like her. And I felt the same." Looking back out the window, he said softly, "Maybe you were right. Maybe I always knew they were wrong for me. And I was glad for the excuse to leave."

Lola swallowed. "But you didn't—"

"Didn't set them up to cheat on me?" He shook his head, his dark eyes luminous in the shadows. "No."

Looking at his face, she believed him.

"Now I have a question for you." Gulping down the last of the Scotch, he set the glass down on the end table. "Is there something you're keeping from me? Some secret?"

"Secret?" She frowned. "I just wanted to know what happened to your engagements. If you were behind the betrayals."

His dark gaze cut into her soul. "Why?"

"Because—" she took a deep breath "—I had to know if you were going to do the same to me."

Rodrigo stared at her. Then he pulled her into his strong arms.

"I will never betray you, Lola." He looked down at her fiercely. "Not in that way, nor any other. When I spoke those vows to you, I meant them." He cupped her cheek. "To love and cherish. For the rest of our lives."

As she stared up at him, feeling the gentle touch of his powerful hand, a rush of relief went through her so great, she almost cried. She hadn't realized until this moment how tense she'd been. How afraid.

"I believe you," she said.

His dark eyes turned warm. "You do?"

"Yes."

His hand moved softly down her neck, through her blond hair, hanging down her shoulders. "I bought you a Christmas present."

"You did?" Just knowing that he hadn't sabotaged his past engagements, and wasn't trying to secretly end their marriage, was all the gift she needed. But he was looking at her so expectantly, she said, "What is it?"

He gave her a wicked smile. "You'll have to wait and see."

"I heard from my sisters today," she blurted out.

He pulled back to look at her, his dark face unreadable. "You did?"

"Well, technically, it was just my youngest sister, Johanna. They sent back the college money, can you believe it? They didn't even want it!" Picking up the check from the floor, she showed him. "They just want us to come for Christmas!"

"Christmas?" he said slowly. "In New York?"

She nodded happily. "Think of it, Rodrigo. Christmas with my sisters, then New Year's Eve with our friends. Cristiano's hosting a party at his new property in Times Square... What do you say?" she rushed out.

Rodrigo stared down at her, his handsome face expressionless. "It's our first Christmas as a family. I thought we'd spend it here. I've made plans..."

"Please." Her voice caught. "You don't know what it means to me that they want to see me."

He looked down at her in the dark, shadowed beach house. "It means so much, *querida*?"

"So much," she whispered.

Rodrigo took a deep breath.

"Then of course we must go."

Joy filled her. With a cry, Lola threw her arms around him, standing on her tiptoes to cover his face with kisses. "You won't regret it!"

Smiling, he murmured, his voice muffled by her kisses, "I'm glad already."

Drawing back, Lola looked up at her husband. The moon's silver light grazed the hard edges of one side, with the lamplight's golden glow on the other. Her heart felt bigger than the world.

And that was when she knew, she really knew, that she loved him.

CHAPTER NINE

IT WAS THE day before Christmas Eve, and the weather had grown cooler, even in Los Angeles. Lola had to wear a soft cotton sweater and jeans instead of a sundress and sandals. But amid the palm trees and California sunshine, as she listened to Christmas songs on the radio about snow and family, all she could think about was their upcoming trip to New York.

Everything was planned. Tomorrow, they'd leave for New York on Rodrigo's private jet, and not return until New Year's Day.

Lola tapped her feet excitedly. Just one more day until she'd finally see her sisters after all these years. She'd done a video chat with them last week, and she could hardly believe how shockingly grown up they looked now. She'd even spoken briefly with their parents. Lola remembered the older couple as guarded, but they seemed warmer now and friendlier.

Perhaps because they weren't scared of her anymore, either. They knew she wasn't a threat to them. She'd never try to fight them for custody or add stress to their lives. How could she? She was grateful to them, for taking the girls into their home as foster kids, then adopting them and giving them such happy lives. When Lola had first seen Johanna and Kelsey's parents seven years ago, she'd been so jealous, she'd hated them, picturing them as entitled and rich.

She knew now that they were just regular people. The father was an engineer. The mother was a school secretary.

Lola had loved seeing pictures of the girls' tidy little house in their picturesque little town, an hour outside New York. Lola had introduced them to Jett in the video chat and shown them pictures of Rodrigo and their beach house in California. Since that time, Johanna kept sending Lola funny pictures of their dog, Peaches, telling her firmly that she "had" to get a dog for Jett, too.

He's not even six months old, Lola had texted back, amused to see her own bossiness manifest in her baby sister.

Jett's my nephew and he needs a dog, Johanna had replied firmly.

Jett had aunts now. More family to love him. And Lola was so grateful.

She'd already wrapped their Christmas presents. The gifts weren't flashy like the college money, expensive and designed to impress, but simple and from the heart. A crystal unicorn for Johanna, who loved anything that was pink and pretty, and an original-press, rare vinyl ABBA album for Kelsey, who was way too young to be a fan, but there you had it. For their parents, she'd bought a pizza stone and accessories, after hearing about their Thursday pizza nights. Even the family dog, Harley, would receive a basket of top-of-the-line homemade dog treats and chew toys.

Lola smiled, just thinking about it.

Jett's Christmas gifts had already been sorted at Thanksgiving, from her and Rodrigo's spree in New York. But she'd spent time writing heartfelt thank-you cards to the housekeepers and bodyguards, to go with their holiday bonuses.

Leaving only one person to shop for. One impossibly difficult person. She'd racked her brain, all the way until today, when it was almost too late.

Until finally, while shopping with the baby today, Lola had had an idea.

Now, as Tobias drove her and Jett back to the beach house in the luxury SUV, Lola leaned back against the soft leather, peeking down at the glossy blue bag in satisfaction. Inside it, she saw a small blue box that held an engraved gold ring.

Finally, her husband would have a wedding band. And when he saw what she'd had engraved inside it...

She shivered. Could she be brave enough?

As the Escalade pulled into the gated courtyard of the beach house, Lola was pulled out of her reverie when she heard Tobias's voice from the front seat. "Mr. Cabrera just sent a message that he's expecting you, ma'am."

"Thank you, Tobias."

She smiled, her heart quickening just at the sound of her husband's name. Since their last argument, the night he'd returned from San Francisco, Rodrigo had taken no more trips away from the family, not even short ones. He'd drastically cut back his hours at work, in a way she'd never seen before. The reason was clear. He wanted to spend time with Jett.

He wanted to spend time with her.

Every morning, he'd stayed late to have breakfast with them, served on the terrace next to the pool. And nearly every evening, he'd been home in time to join them for dinner, then help with the baby's bath. On weekends, they'd gone on family excursions, Disneyland, hiking trails in the nearby hills, visiting art museums and the zoo and the farmer's market, even boating to Catalina Island. All normal things that any family might do. Well, except for the fact that Rodrigo owned the yacht that took them to Catalina.

But tonight, he'd hinted, before they left for New York, he had something extra special planned.

"Not just for Christmas," he'd told her that morning,

nuzzling her in bed. He'd drawn back to give her a serious look as he said huskily, "For always."

All day, Lola had tried not to think of what it could mean. So of course it was all she could think about.

Now, as Tobias parked the car, she asked suddenly, "How's your son doing?"

"Great." The bodyguard grinned. "Both of us are great, Mrs. Cabrera. Thanks to you."

"Good." As he got out to open her car door, Lola lingered over the seat belt of her baby's car seat.

Please. She fervently closed her eyes. *Please let Rodrigo's surprise be him telling me he loves me.*

Because she loved him. It was always on the tip of her tongue now. Every time she watched him tenderly hold their baby. Every evening they spent together on the poolside terrace at sunset, drinking a glass of wine after Jett was asleep. Every night he took Lola to bed and moved his hot, sensual body against hers until he set her world on fire.

She loved him. She wanted to scream it to the world. She wanted to look into his rugged features and speak the words, again and again, like a sacred incantation.

Then she wanted him to say the words back to her.

Please, she thought. She didn't want any expensive gifts for Christmas. She didn't want anything but this: for her husband to love her.

"Mrs. Cabrera?"

Pasting a smile on her face, Lola lifted her baby out of the car seat. Walking to the front door of the sprawling beach house, she looked up at the tall, slender palm trees, swaying in the wind, silhouetted purple against the lowering sun in the orange and red horizon.

Squaring her shoulders, she carried the baby to the front door, her footsteps echoing against the flagstones. She opened the door.

And gasped.

The great room of the beach house, with its luxurious furniture and double-story window views of the Pacific, had been filled with roses of every color, hundreds of them, pink and red and yellow and white. But that wasn't even the most amazing part.

Rodrigo stood beside the doorway, devastatingly attractive in a tuxedo, holding out a long-stemmed pink rose.

Lola's heart slammed against her ribs. Her hand shook as she took the rose. "What's this?"

He gave her a wicked smile. "Christmas."

"It's not even Christmas Eve yet."

"Tomorrow's for family." His dark eyes gleamed down at her. "Tonight's for us."

"For us?" A flash of heat went through her, and her cheeks burned. "I thought we'd be getting a Christmas tree tonight."

"We are. In a way." He allowed himself a smug smile, then glanced behind him. "Mrs. Lee will be watching Jett."

The housekeeper came forward, smiling as she took the baby from Lola's arms. "Have a nice evening, Mrs. Cabrera."

"But—where are we going?"

"Go to our bedroom," Rodrigo said, his dark eyes burning through her.

"Now?"

"Right now."

Going down the hall to the palatial master bedroom, Lola dropped her shopping bag in shock when she saw a famous personal stylist waiting for her, with two makeup and hair stylists.

"Hello." The personal stylist, who dressed movie stars for worldwide events, gave Lola a cheeky smile. "I'm here for you, my dear. To make you even more impossibly beautiful than you already are." He motioned toward a rack of ball gowns and brand-new designer shoes. "Choose your favorite. They're all in your size." He held up a sleek, well-used sewing kit and double-sided tape. "I can make any gown fit."

Thirty minutes later, Lola felt so ridiculously like a princess, she was sure even Johanna would approve. Looking in the full-length mirror, Lola hardly recognized herself.

Her long, highlighted blond hair was sleek and perfect, falling nearly to her waist. Her strapless pink chiffon gown fit her perfectly, showing off her curves. Black kohl and fake eyelashes lined her eyes, making the hazel color pop dramatically, and her lips were pink.

Standing in the sparkling six-inch designer heels, Lola breathed, "I don't even need jewelry."

The stylist gave her a wicked grin. "You sparkle enough on your own."

"I feel like Cinderella," she said.

"You look like her, too." He tilted his head. "You married the most powerful man in showbiz, girl. This city, this world, is yours to command."

Lola felt like she was in a dream as she walked back down the hall in the strapless pink chiffon gown. Even the six-inch heels felt fantastic on her feet, as if she were floating on air. She'd never had a problem with designer heels making her feet hurt. They were too beautiful—too expensive—to hurt.

But what were they doing tonight?

Lola looked down at the glamorous pink gown. Obviously, not going Christmas tree shopping.

When she returned to the great room, the housekeeper and Jett were gone. Rodrigo stood alone amid the roses.

His eyes widened when he saw her.

"Querida," he whispered. "You take my breath away."

"Thanks." Coming forward shyly, she reached up to straighten his black tie. "You don't clean up so badly yourself."

"I bought you some Christmas decorations."

"Mistletoe?" she guessed.

"I should have thought of that. But no." Pulling a black, flat velvet box from his tuxedo jacket pocket, he held it out. Lola sucked in her breath when she saw a magnificent diamond necklace, sparkling in the twilight, amid all the sweet-scented roses.

"Oh," she whispered.

"Hold up your hair," he said huskily.

She did as he commanded. Dropping the black velvet box on an antique side table, he placed the diamonds around her neck, attaching the clasp behind her.

The necklace felt cold and heavy against Lola's skin. But the feather-light brush of his fingertips as he hooked the clasp sent a flash of fire through her body.

"There." Turning her to face him, he stroked her cheek, tilting her head upward. "*Now* you are ready."

Lola looked up at him, her heart thudding in her chest. *I love you, Rodrigo.* The words lifted to her throat. Her lips parted—

"Don't look at me like that, *querida.*" He gave a low, rueful laugh. "If you do, I'll cancel our plans tonight, and spend the next twelve hours with you in bed."

"Would that be so horrible?"

"No…and yes." He gave her a wicked grin. "Because I have something very special planned for you."

"Are we exchanging our Christmas gifts tonight?"

"Maybe," he said huskily. "Except my gift to you can't be wrapped. Something I know—" his eyes met hers "—is your heart's desire."

Joy pounded through her, making her dizzy. *He was going to tell her he loved her.* Tonight. She blurted, "I have something for you, too."

Turning, she raced back to the master bedroom, where the stylists were packing up clothes and beauty supplies.

Finding her bag from the jewelry store, she pulled out the gold wedding band she'd bought as his Christmas gift. She glanced at its inscription: *I love you now and always.*

But where could she hide it until the right moment? Biting her lip, she looked around desperately. "Is there a handbag to match my dress?"

"There's always a bag," the stylist said lazily. He narrowed his eyes, then gave a satisfied nod and handed her an adorable pink minaudière laced with pink crystals. Hastily, she tucked her phone, ID, a lipstick and a bit of cash inside. She felt bright with happiness. "Wait," the stylist said, wrapping a pink stole around her shoulders. "Take this. It's cold out."

When she returned to the great room, Rodrigo came closer, dark-haired and devastating in his sleek tuxedo. Lifting her hand to his lips, he kissed it, causing her to shiver as ripples of electricity and heat whipped through her body.

"Tonight, I want to fulfill all your dreams," he said seriously, wrapping her hand over his arm.

Lola's heart was pounding as he led her outside, where she saw his red two-seater Ferrari waiting. She tried to tell herself to calm down but couldn't. She felt like she was in a dream as he helped her into the passenger seat.

After starting the engine, Rodrigo drove past the beach house's gate and onto the coastal highway, heading east, into the sprawl of Los Angeles.

When they reached the outskirts of Beverly Hills, traveling a winding road past all the hidden mansions with their gates and fortress-like hedges, a sudden suspicion began to grow inside her.

"Where are we going?" she asked.

Rodrigo shook his head, a smile quirking his sensual lips. Then he turned into a driveway blocked by an elaborate wrought iron gate. Words were worked into the top of the tall gate: La Casa del Corazón.

"What are we doing here?" She turned to her husband, eyes wide. "Is there a party?"

"You might say that." Reaching out of his window, Rodrigo punched in a code on the security keypad, causing the electronic gate to smoothly slide open. The car continued up the sweeping driveway. To her surprise, Lola saw cars parked along the short private road, all the way to the massive circular driveway around a Spanish-style stone fountain. Parking directly in front of the lavish mansion, he turned off the engine.

He turned to face her, his dark eyes shining.

"The house of your dreams." Taking her hand, he put a key into her palm. "It's yours."

She blinked. "What?"

"It wasn't on the market." He gave her a quietly proud smile. "But you told me you wanted it, so I made the owners an offer they couldn't refuse."

Lola looked up at the stunning 1920s-era Spanish Mediterranean mansion. Built by silent film stars a hundred years before, this home was a rare beauty, an architectural landmark. Tears lifted to her eyes.

It wasn't that he'd bought her a mansion. They already had one of those, a nice one on the beach.

It was that Rodrigo had listened. When she'd told him her youthful dreams, he hadn't mocked them. He hadn't forgotten. He'd tried to make them come true.

"But why are we dressed up like this?" she said, blinking fast. "And why are there so many cars? I don't understand."

His smile widened. "There's more."

"More?"

Searching his gaze, she caught her breath. He'd brought her family and friends here, she thought suddenly. Since they hadn't been at the wedding. He was going to tell her he loved her tonight, in front of everyone she cared about, in front of Hallie and Tess and their families. In front of her sisters. The certainty, the overwhelming romance of the moment filled her.

And suddenly, she couldn't wait. Fear disappeared, along with pride.

Lola let him see her heart. She didn't even try to hide the joyful tears suddenly falling down her cheeks.

Looking up at him as he sat beside her in the Ferrari, she whispered, "I love you, Rodrigo."

He blinked. He said slowly, "You love the house—"

"No. You." She lifted her hand to his rough cheek. "Not your money. Not these diamonds—" she glanced down at her necklace "—not even this beautiful house. I love you," she said fiercely. Shaking her head, she smiled through her tears. "I don't think I've ever stopped loving you. From the night we first kissed. All this time. Even when there was no hope."

His gaze shuttered. "Lola—"

"I told you I was only marrying you for Jett's sake. But it was a lie. I was scared to admit the truth, even to myself. But I can't deny it any longer." Taking a deep breath, she whispered, "I love you. Only you. And I'll love you forever."

She couldn't mean it.

Lola…loved him?

A horrifying flash of memories raced through Rodrigo of three other women speaking those exact same words, with the same apparent sincerity—right before they slept with another, with his engagement ring still on their fingers.

Only fools put faith in love. Fools and masochists. If he let himself love her, he knew how this would end.

And yet… His heart cried out for her.

He wanted to believe. His long-ago engagements felt like nothing—just the hasty, shallow infatuations of a young man—compared to what he felt for her now.

The thought shocked him.

Rodrigo's gaze fell to the diamond engagement ring gleaming on Lola's left hand. He couldn't let himself love her. What if she betrayed him?

No. He took a shuddering breath. He couldn't live through it. It would destroy him.

Rodrigo forced himself to give her a casual, crooked smile. "Lola, you don't need to say you love me. I've already bought you the house. You can relax."

Lola's beautiful face, which had been hopeful and bright, closed up instantly. He felt an answering wrench in his chest that almost made him sick.

He knew she wasn't pretending or buttering him up. She actually believed she loved him.

But he also knew it wouldn't—couldn't—last. He could not take the chance of loving her. They were married. They had a child. There was too much at stake to risk it on something so deceitful and destructive as love.

His jaw tightened. "We have guests. We should go inside."

"Guests?" she said, with a tiny sliver of hope in her voice. "What guests?"

"It's part of your surprise. A housewarming party."

"Who did you invite?"

"Everyone."

Her eyes lit up. "My sisters? My friends?"

Rodrigo suddenly wished he had. He should have invited the Morettis and Zaccos and those sisters of hers. It hadn't even occurred to him.

"No," he said quietly. "Industry people."

The light in her eyes faded. "Oh."

Looking down at her, he felt it again, that punch in the gut. And all of his Christmas plans he'd been arranging for weeks with Marnie, the mansion he'd been so excited to give his wife tonight as a surprise, suddenly seemed meaningless and cheap.

His shoulders tightened in his tuxedo jacket. Getting heavily out of the car, he opened her door. Holding out his hand, he said, "Come."

Her hand shook as she placed it in his. She wouldn't meet his eyes. As they entered the house's glittering foyer, beneath the wrought iron Spanish chandelier high above, he felt a ragged blade in his throat.

"Mr. Cabrera!" Marnie McAdam strode toward them in black stilettos, her skinny frame swathed in a black sheath dress. "You're here!" She looked at him happily, then glanced at Lola. "Mrs. Cabrera, I hope you like your party."

There was a strange note of satisfaction in Marnie's voice that Rodrigo didn't understand.

She's just being a good assistant, he told himself. Marnie cared so much about her job, of course she wanted to make sure his wife has a good time. And yet it struck Rodrigo as odd.

Then he looked around them.

The enormous grand foyer, framed by a sweeping wrought iron staircase on each side, was filled with the most powerful people in the entertainment and media worlds: studio heads, directors and movie stars. He'd invited them because he wanted to properly introduce Lola, not as his assistant, but as his wife—to gain their respect for her as a power in her own right.

But now, as he glanced at Lola on his arm, Rodrigo realized his mistake.

The Spanish-style mansion was decorated in glamorous Christmas finery, with holly and ivy draped along the wrought iron handrails of the dual staircases. In the center of the enormous foyer, a twenty-foot Christmas tree was decorated with sparkling ornaments and lights glittering like stars. Beneath the tree was a veritable Himalayan mountain range of gifts, all for Lola and the baby, elegantly wrapped in red, as the decorator had arranged for maximum effect.

For weeks now, Rodrigo had imagined Lola's face when she saw this. He'd been determined to give her everything she'd once dreamed of when she'd come to this city at eighteen, broke and alone.

But now, Lola's beautiful face was sad. Her big hazel eyes looked heartbroken and numb. He'd never seen her look so vulnerable. Her lovely face still was tracked with dried tears, from when she'd told him she loved him just moments before, when she'd been crying with joy.

And now, of all times, he was forcing her to face judgmental strangers, his business partners and rivals. Now, at the very moment he'd hurt her so badly.

Rodrigo suddenly hated this stupid party. And this stupid house. He wished he'd never thought of this gift. He would have given anything to have the two of them back at the beach house. Alone.

All the people in formal gowns and tuxedos, drinking expensive champagne, turned toward them with a cheer.

"To Mr. and Mrs. Cabrera!" someone cried from the back, and everyone held up champagne flutes.

"Congratulations!" The shout rang across the enormous foyer.

"You did it, old man!" laughed a hot young filmmaker, barely out of USC film school, holding up his flute.

"And Merry Christmas!" cried someone else. "Wishing us all fat profits in this happy season!"

Lola suddenly burst into tears.

"Excuse me," she choked out, covering her face.

"Lola, wait," Rodrigo said desperately, but she ran out of the foyer. He tried to follow but found his passage blocked by ten different people, all of them coming forward to congratulate him—that was to say, determined to network with the powerful Spanish film mogul in hopes of getting their various projects made.

"Don't worry, sir." Standing beside him, Marnie flashed a sympathetic look. "I'll go check on her."

He tossed her a glance. "No, wait—"

But his assistant was already gone.

Five minutes, he told himself grimly. He'd let Lola have five minutes to gather herself. He'd never seen her sob like that before. He knew her pride. She wouldn't want him to see.

But he'd already seen the tears overflowing her lashes. Just as he'd already seen her vulnerable heart.

I love you, she'd whispered. *Only you. And I'll love you forever.*

"And in the spirit of Christmas, Cabrera—" a Hollywood power agent was saying eagerly, pumping his hand "—I'll let you read my client's screenplay. You're a lucky bastard, because it's truly spectacular—"

Screw five minutes, Rodrigo thought. He couldn't wait. He couldn't know Lola was somewhere, crying alone, while he did nothing to comfort her. It was unbearable. He had to protect her. Comfort her. He had to make it right.

"Excuse me," he said to the agent as he droned about his client's high-concept plot. "I have to find my wife."

Without waiting for a response, he turned and pushed his way through the crowds of glamorous, wealthy guests, in the direction Lola had disappeared. Suddenly, Marnie blocked his path. Her thin face was anxious and worried.

"There's an uninvited guest."

"Take care of it," he told her harshly. "I need to find Lola."

But as he impatiently started to pass her, his assistant stopped him with a tug at his arm. "It's Sergei Morozov."

His wife's old boss from New York? The Russian tycoon

who'd wanted to marry her? That grabbed Rodrigo's attention. He scowled at Marnie. "He wasn't on the guest list."

"No. Somehow he snuck in."

Rodrigo took a deep breath, trying to shake off the sudden tension in his shoulders. What could Morozov be doing here, three thousand miles from New York? Old fears started to creep in. Could Lola have…?

No. He thought of the emotion shining in his wife's hazel eyes when she told him she loved him. Lola would never cheat on him. He trusted her, as he trusted no one else.

"Let the man stay. I don't care," he said suddenly. He turned away. "I need to find my wife—"

"That's just it, sir." Marnie stopped him with her solemn, owl-like gaze. "I'm trying to tell you. Mr. Morozov is here. He's with Mrs. Cabrera." She hesitated, then said, "They're *together.*"

Rodrigo frowned, unable to make sense of his assistant's words. "Together?"

She bit her lip. "In the back garden. I saw them. Kissing—"

Marnie kept talking, but suddenly Rodrigo couldn't hear her.

As he looked around the foyer, all the people talking and laughing and drinking champagne suddenly seemed like mere noise to Rodrigo, just smudges of color.

He had no memory of how he walked through the crowds to the French doors overlooking the terrace. He'd only remember the feeling of wading through air like water, feeling like he couldn't breathe.

Outside in the cold air, he heard his assistant behind him as he walked across the Spanish terrace, looking out into the manicured tropical gardens, lush beneath the moonlight.

But he saw nothing. No one.

Waves of relief went over him. There was no one here.

Reason returned to his brain and he started to turn back to Marnie. "You were mistaken—"

Then he saw a gleam of pink chiffon from the corner of his eye. A flash of Lola's long blond hair.

And Rodrigo saw, in the shadows on the other side of the terrace, the sickening sight of another man embracing his wife.

"Do not worry, *zvezda moya*," he heard the Russian croon, holding Lola tenderly in his arms. "You are safe now. With me."

CHAPTER TEN

SHOCKED, LOLA STRUGGLED in her old boss's arms.

A moment before, she'd run out on the dark, empty terrace to sob alone, when a man had suddenly appeared from the shadows. At first, she'd thought it was Rodrigo, and unwilling hope had risen in her heart. Then she'd recognized her old boss, Sergei Morozov.

"Sergei? What are you doing here?" she'd said in surprise, choking back her tears.

"What has he done to you, *Lolitchka*?" he'd said indignantly. "Look at you. Crying. He did this?"

She'd shaken her head vehemently. "No, he—" Then she'd stopped. Because Rodrigo was exactly the reason why she was out here crying alone.

No. That wasn't fair. He'd told her all along not to love him. Just like he had during the months of their first affair. And just like she had then, she'd let herself care for him anyway.

Only this was so much worse. Because she truly loved him. And she didn't know how she'd ever be able to face him again, knowing all he felt for her in return was pity.

She'd done this to herself.

Wiping her eyes, she'd said to Sergei, "Did Rodrigo invite you here? Are you friends now?"

"Friends?" Sergei's eyes had flashed. "No. This man you married, he sent me a message. Inviting me to take you."

Lola had frowned. There must be something lost in translation. "Take me? Take me where?"

"Away from him." He'd snorted. "I do not understand how he could so easily tire of you. Now I, I would not so quickly tire. But I do not question. I am here. I gladly take."

"Take?" she'd said, backing away until her heels hit the mansion's stucco wall, trapping her.

"Da," he'd said huskily. "His email said we must be seen together. Then he pays nothing to end the marriage."

"What?" she'd gasped in shock, staring at him. "He would never say that!"

She'd heard a French door open, as someone came out on the moonswept terrace. Grateful to have someone else there, to stop her old boss's apparent madness, she turned to see who it was—

"Do not worry, *zvezda moya*." His eyes gleamed. Grabbing her suddenly with his big arms, he yanked her hard against him. "You are safe now. With me."

"What? Stop!" Lola struggled in his arms, breaking away just in time to see who'd come out on the terrace.

Rodrigo.

His handsome face looked pale beneath his tanned, olive-toned skin, his dark eyes black as death as he stared at her. In another man's arms.

"No." Lola breathed, realizing what it must look like, after all the times he'd been betrayed. "No, Rodrigo, wait! It's not what you think!"

But her husband didn't wait. Without a word, he turned on his heel and went back inside the house.

Lingering behind him on the terrace, Lola saw his assistant, Marnie, staring at her smugly. Then she, too, turned and left.

"Sergei," Lola gasped, shoving him away. "Why did you do that?"

He frowned. "You do not like?"

"Of course I don't! What gave you the impression that I would?"

"But I thought you were a gold digger. Why not me instead of him?" He pounded his chest. "When I grow tired of you, I will openly give you a divorce! With money!"

Gripping her pink-crystal minaudière, Lola shook her head tearfully. "I love my husband. I would never, ever betray him!"

The man's expression changed. "I am sorry. I did not know." He looked after Rodrigo. "Sadly, he does not feel the same."

With a tearful glance, she rushed to follow her husband into the Beverly Hills mansion. She pushed through the crowds, desperate to find him, but she could not.

Finally, she ran out into the front courtyard, by the burbling stone fountain. She came out just in time to see Rodrigo driving away.

Desperately, she ran out in front of him, blocking the Ferrari's path. "Stop!"

Rodrigo's black eyes pierced through her, filled with anger. "Get out of my way, Lola."

"Not until you let me in this car!"

His voice was cold. "Your funeral."

Lola half expected him to drive off and leave her as soon as she was no longer blocking his path. But he let her climb into the passenger seat beside him. Without looking at her, he stomped on the gas.

They drove away from their own party, from their new Beverly Hills mansion, from all the guests and gifts and everything else.

She stared at her husband in the moonlight. His eyes remained stubbornly on the road, as if she weren't there. But she saw the way his jaw twitched, saw how tightly his hands gripped the steering wheel.

Lola took a deep breath.

"Please," she whispered. "You can't think—"

"Can't think what?" he bit out, his voice dangerously low. "Can't think the woman who claimed to love me betrayed me for another?"

"I know that it might have looked like that, but I never—"

He gave a low bitter laugh. "I know what I saw."

"You don't!"

He flashed her a glance, his dark eyes like ice. "Then what did I see?"

"Sergei said someone sent him an email, pretending to be you. Inviting him to take me. Practically begging him to."

"What do you mean, *take you*?"

"But I know it wasn't you," she whispered. "I know you wouldn't do something so underhanded and dishonorable."

"No. *I* wouldn't." He turned right, taking the corner too fast.

"Neither would I. Because I love you—"

"Stop it." His eyes narrowed as he stared at the road. "You invited him to the party tonight. Admit it."

"How could I? I didn't know about it!"

"You must have found out somehow," he muttered. Looking at his tight posture, at the way he stared so fiercely at the road, she felt the waves of misery coming off his body, and her heart broke for him.

Lola thought rapidly. If she hadn't invited Sergei, and Rodrigo hadn't either, then who? Who would have anything to gain by wrecking their marriage?

Every time Rodrigo gets close to a woman, he sabotages it. I used to blame myself, but not anymore. Not after it happened in all three of his engagements.

If Rodrigo hadn't sabotaged all his relationships, then who had? Who had the ability, and the reason?

Lola sucked in her breath.

Suddenly, she knew.

"It was Marnie," she choked out. "She did it. All of it."

Rodrigo scowled as he drove. "What are you talking about?"

Lola stared at him. In the window behind him, she could see tall palm trees turn silver in the moonlight. "Marnie invited Sergei tonight."

"Now you're blaming my assistant for your own unfaithfulness?" He gave a bitter laugh. "You must be truly desperate."

"It's the only thing that makes sense!"

He glanced at her coldly. "And why would she?"

She thought fast. "Marnie wanted you for herself," she said slowly. "So she's systematically rid herself of any rival who crossed her path."

"That's ridiculous. I've known her for over a decade."

"Exactly."

He gave a harsh laugh. "*Marnie* forced all my fiancées to cheat?"

"She's your assistant. She has access to everything. Your email. Your bank accounts. She could hire actors and pay them directly. She could even arrange for pictures to be sent to you as evidence."

"Because she's wildly in love with me." His tone dripped sarcasm.

She glared at him. "Don't you think it's a strange coincidence that you happened to come out on the terrace the *exact moment* Sergei grabbed me?"

For a moment, Rodrigo looked at her blankly. Then he narrowed his eyes. "Stop it."

"It's the only explanation!"

"Marnie McAdam had been loyal to me for years. I won't let you insult her." His voice was low, savage. "Not to assuage your own guilt."

"But—"

"Not another word. I mean it."

His body was vibrating with repressed fury. He didn't believe her.

With an angry breath, Lola turned away, looking out at the moonswept night as they drove past a charming commercial street. The palm trees were decked with white lights, the elegant restaurants and boutiques draped in artificial snow. It all felt so fake. Her heart hurt.

Living in the high desert as a child, there'd been no palm trees, just sagebrush and scrubby Joshua trees, and dirt yards instead of manicured green lawns. But at least that had been real. She would have preferred that, she thought with a lump in her throat, to this.

"Please, Rodrigo," she whispered, trying one last time. "Think about it. She had to have arranged it—"

Pulling the Ferrari abruptly to the curb, Rodrigo turned to her, his black eyes hard. "Get out."

"What?" She breathed in shock. She looked at his taut shoulders, his cold features. Shivering, she looked out at the trendy neighborhood, at the sleek, expensive apartment buildings on one side, and the luxury car dealership on the other. "You can't mean it."

"You lied to me." His dark eyes were like ice. Like an enemy staring at her over the barrel of a gun. "I want you out of my life. For good."

"You're not seriously going to leave me here?"

His low, hateful voice cut through her. "Get. Out."

With her heart bleeding inside her, Lola clung to her pride. It was all she had left. Slowly, she opened the car door. Gripping her pink-crystal clutch, she turned back to him, hating the begging in her voice but unable to stop herself. "Please, Rodrigo, please, if you'll only listen—"

But he didn't even look at her. The open door slipped out of her hands as he pressed hard on the gas, driving away from her without another word, or another look.

Lola watched the car drive away from her, leaving her abandoned on a corner of Santa Monica Boulevard, the old Route 66. She couldn't believe he'd left. Despair filled her as she clutched her pink stole over her shoulders, shivering in the cooling air. Fighting tears, she reached into her bag for her phone.

Then she saw it. The gold wedding band she'd planned to give him tonight. With the inscription *I love you now and always.*

Her eyes widened, and she fell to pieces. A sob racked through her, and she covered her face with her hands.

Her husband was gone. Everything was gone.

No. Not everything.

Lola looked up from her hands with an intake of breath. *Her baby.*

Fighting down emotion, she wiped her eyes hard. Finding her phone, she dialed with shaking hands. She waited as the line rang and rang. When the other person finally picked up, she nearly cried with relief.

"Please," she whispered. "Please help me."

Rodrigo felt nothing as he drove away. He felt numb, from the inside out.

As he drove up the coast, his phone rang repeatedly. Sure that it was Lola, he ignored it. Let her find her own way home. She had a phone. She had credit cards. Let her get a taxi. Or, hell, he'd abandoned her in front of a car dealership—let her buy herself one and drive herself home.

He wouldn't be at the beach house when she got there.

A woman had cheated on him. *Again.* And not just a fiancée this time.

He'd been betrayed by his wife. His partner. The mother of his child. The woman he—

Rodrigo's stomach twisted. He glanced out at the sweep of moonlight against the black ocean. He should have known better than to trust her. He should have known better than to care.

Stopping at a traffic light, he cursed loudly, punching the dashboard. As he clawed back his hair, he saw the people in the next car staring at him in alarm. As soon as the light turned green, they drove away in a terrified puff of smoke.

No wonder they were afraid. He probably looked like a madman. But the truth was worse.

He was cursed. Cursed from childhood.

His own mother hadn't loved him, his biological father hadn't claimed him, and the man who'd given him the Cabrera name had despised him. Rodrigo had been desperate from childhood to find someone to love.

But he hadn't.

And he wouldn't.

He would never love anyone. Or be loved in return.

A chill went through him, like the sudden frigid calm that came over someone sinking into icy waters for the last time.

Whatever. He set his jaw. He didn't need it. He didn't need Lola, either. He'd forget her, just like all the rest.

Except she wasn't like the rest.

Their relationship hadn't begun with flowers and fancy televised awards shows, or amid the fantasy of a big screen dream, but quietly, slowly over time. He and Lola had been partners first, then friends, and finally lovers.

He knew her. He trusted her.

Or at least he *had*.

That was what made her betrayal the worst of all.

Swallowing against the lump in his throat, he tightened his grip on the steering wheel. He'd make her regret it. He'd fight for custody of Jett. Whatever the prenuptial agreement had promised, Lola didn't deserve custody of their son. She was corrupt, deceitful, a horrible excuse for a human being. She was no fit mother—

Memories of all her hours caring for their baby, so lovingly and so well, ripped through him. All her time and care had gone to their son, while his own hours had often been spent building his business empire.

Would he really hurt Jett, by taking him from the care of a loving mother, to leave him instead with paid nannies, as Rodrigo had once been? Could he be so determined to punish his wife that he'd hurt his son as collateral damage?

Furiously, he set his jaw. Fine. He'd let Lola keep custody. But he'd take everything else. The prenuptial agreement was watertight. If she cheated, she ended up with nothing. She should enjoy buying that car from the dealership tonight. She wouldn't have it long.

When he finally pulled past the gate into the courtyard of his beach house, he parked haphazardly. He had to take a deep breath before he picked up his phone. But to his shock, he saw it hadn't been Lola calling, but Marnie. She'd left several messages.

She was probably worried, after he'd abandoned his own party without an explanation. But Marnie had seen what happened on the terrace. She didn't need one.

Rodrigo stared up blankly at his beach house.

How could Lola have betrayed him? How?

Had she lied when she told him she loved him?

I love you. He heard the echo of her tender whisper. *Only you. And I'll love you forever.*

He felt sick, remembering. If she loved him, how could she have immediately betrayed him?

Had she been so crushed by Rodrigo's rejection of her love that she'd immediately jumped into the arms of another man? And she'd somehow invited Sergei Morozov to the party beforehand?

But that didn't make sense. He remembered Lola's shock when she'd first seen the magnificent Spanish-style mansion. She hadn't known about the party.

Then who?

Marnie wanted you for herself. So she's systematically rid herself of any rival who crossed her path.

No. He shook his head angrily. Sweet, loyal Marnie, who'd devoted nearly fifteen years to his service? No, impossible. He wasn't going to listen to Lola's excuses or impossible story.

Perhaps Morozov had been stalking Lola all this time. Perhaps the investigator had been wrong, and the two of them had continued to secretly be in contact after her marriage. And tonight, when her pride was wounded, she'd immediately phoned the other man, telling him she wanted him—

It didn't matter. Going inside the beach house, Rodrigo slammed the door behind him. He would send for his lawyers at once. But first, he had to see his son. Right now. He had to feel like there was still one thing on earth he could depend on. One person he could love, who loved him back.

But the house was dark and empty. Feeling cold, Rodrigo walked through it, calling the housekeeper's name. But the kitchen was dark.

So was the nursery. The crib was empty.

His son.

Snatching up his phone, he frantically dialed his housekeeper's number, then his bodyguard's. If Tobias didn't pick up, he'd call the police—

He nearly gasped with relief when the line was answered.

"Jett's fine, Mr. Cabrera," Tobias replied calmly. "He's safe here in the car. With his mother."

Rodrigo's jaw dropped. "Lola is with you?"

"Yes. I'm driving Mrs. Cabrera to the airport now. She's taking the first flight back to New York."

To New York.

Gripping his phone, Rodrigo looked slowly around the

shadowy beach house. Outside, the silvery moonlight on the vast, black Pacific seemed hollow and gray.

"She called me after you abandoned her on the side of the road." His bodyguard's voice was reproachful. "That was cold, Mr. Cabrera. God knows I hate my ex, but even I wouldn't do that."

Let me talk to her, Rodrigo wanted to say. Then he remembered how he'd told her he wanted her out of his life for good. How he'd left her standing on the sidewalk in Santa Monica. Lola would never forgive him for that. Ever. Even if he'd wanted her to.

"You don't have to fire me for it, either," Tobias said. "Because I qu—"

"You're not fired," Rodrigo said heavily.

The man paused. "I'm not?"

"You're right," he said flatly. "My son should be with his mother. Lola knows how to love him. I don't. Take them to the airport. And leave me the hell alone."

Rodrigo hung up. Grabbing a bottle of whiskey—not tequila, never tequila, it would only remind him of Mexico City—he drank it straight from the bottle.

He drank through Christmas Eve, until Christmas finally came, bright and fine. The sun sparkled in the blue sky, shimmering against the wide ocean, which stretched out forever.

Just like his empty beach house. Once, Rodrigo had thought this house was the perfect size. Perfect for dating, perfect for entertaining and impressing others.

Now, it stretched with the vast emptiness of space, lacking oxygen, leaving him to float, with nothing to cling to. Especially after Mrs. Lee arrived to pack up all of Lola and Jett's things and mail them to Hallie Moretti's house in the West Village.

The day after Christmas, Rodrigo put the whiskey away. He forced himself to get up. To shave. To shower. To run ten miles along the beach, then visit a boxing gym, where he punched the hell out of everything.

For the rest of the week, he focused on work, ordering his whole team to come back into the office early, in order to greenlight production of as many new films as possible. If anyone on his staff dared voice a single regret at giving up their holidays with their families, Rodrigo verbally ripped them apart. He didn't need a family. Why should they?

He was better off alone. They would be, too.

By midafternoon on New Year's Eve, Rodrigo was holed up in his luxurious private office in the Cabrera Media Group headquarters in downtown Los Angeles, staring at his computer, manically reading script after script. He'd been there all night, sleeping fitfully on the sofa in his office. He planned to do the same tonight for New Year's Eve. As long as he kept working, there'd be no need for him to return to the beach house. Ever.

Or think about the divorce papers his lawyers had prepared for him, already waiting at his house for his signature.

Marnie, who all week had seemed as nervous of him as a caged tiger, peeked into his office. "Mr. Cabrera?"

Impatiently, Rodrigo waved her in. "You have my clothes?"

"Yes, sir." She handed him the duffel bag of clean clothes she'd brought from his beach house.

Grabbing it, he turned away. "Thanks."

"Are you doing all right, sir?"

"Of course I'm all right." He glared at her. "I'm not like my board, whining about their families and the holiday season. They have no work ethic." He took a deep breath, controlling his tone. "But you do, Marnie. You haven't complained once. Thank you for that."

"I'm glad to be here, sir." She set down a stack of papers on his large dark wood desk. "Ned Stone sent over a script. He says it's a four-quadrant film."

Ned Stone was the biggest agent in Hollywood, and a four-quadrant film was the holy grail of the film industry: a movie that would appeal to both men and women, young and old.

But looking at it, Rodrigo didn't feel elated. He just felt tired. So tired, in fact, the room seemed to swim in front of his eyes.

"Take it back," he whispered, not moving. "I don't want it."

Marnie stared at him, her eyebrows lifted in shock. "You don't care about a four-quadrant film?"

"No," he said slowly. "I don't."

Since Lola had left, he'd tried to lose himself in work. He'd committed hundreds of millions of dollars to projects he couldn't even remember now. Half his board was threatening to quit and muttering dark suspicions about his mental health. But for all that, he felt exhausted and numb. Hollow.

He'd tried to run away from his feelings. He'd tried not to think of Lola. But he'd failed. She was all he could think about. He hated work. He hated home. Most of all, he hated himself.

Because without his wife, nothing else mattered. Not success, not fame or fortune. Not even a four-quadrant film.

Because he loved her.

Rodrigo felt a *whoosh* go through his body, like vertigo. He staggered back beneath the weight of the realization. The duffel bag slid from his hands to the hardwood floor.

Oh, my God. *He loved her.*

All this time, he'd tried to keep his heart cold. But he'd been lying to himself. The truth was, in the depths of his heart, he'd known it was already too late. He'd loved her from the moment she'd kissed him in Mexico City. Perhaps even before.

That was why he'd never slept with another woman. His body had known what his mind and heart refused to admit. He'd been too afraid to admit it, even to himself, after all the times he'd been hurt by the women he'd loved.

Except he hadn't loved his first three fiancées, he now realized. How could he? He'd barely known them. As a young man, he'd been so desperate for love, to have a real family, that he'd proposed marriage within weeks.

Then he'd promptly come up with a reason to leave. Because he hadn't loved those three women, any more than they'd loved him. If they had, they wouldn't have been so easily lured away.

But he loved Lola. It had terrified him. Seeing her in Morozov's arms had been all the excuse he needed to end their relationship. He'd almost been relieved to accept the worst rather than let himself be vulnerable, and love her.

But Lola, who'd also known pain and loss, hadn't given in to fear. She'd been brave. She'd been loyal. She'd had his back, all along.

Get this through your head, she'd said. *I'll never betray you, Rodrigo. Ever.*

And she hadn't.

Rodrigo was the one who'd betrayed her.

"Are you all right, sir?" Marnie frowned, coming closer in the downtown office. "You don't look well."

His jaw clenched. He'd betrayed Lola by not trusting her, when she'd been the best friend he'd ever had. He'd betrayed her by not being brave enough to give his heart.

"Sir?"

He slowly looked at his assistant.

And he'd betrayed his wife by not believing her, when she was the smartest person he knew.

Marnie wanted you for herself. So she's systematically rid herself of any rival who crossed her path. She's your assistant. She has access to everything.

"Marnie," he said quietly. "I know what you did."

His assistant's eyes widened beneath her thick glasses. Then, slowly, she smiled. "I've just acted as any good secretary would. And kept my boss out of trouble."

Ice went down his spine. Lola had been right about everything. "You sabotaged my engagements."

Marnie's eyes turned bright, eager. "It wasn't even hard. They all fell for it so easily. They cheated. They proved they weren't worthy of you."

He felt sick.

"But Lola didn't."

She scowled. "I sent the best porn actor from the agency. But she blew him off. I had to be more creative."

"So you sent the message to Morozov, pretending to be me."

"I knew you couldn't actually want to be married to her." Her expression darkened. "She doesn't love you. Not like I do."

I love you. The memory of Lola's beautiful face, her luminous hazel eyes in the moonlit night, came back to him. *Only you. And I'll love you forever.*

"I did it all for you." Marnie's thin face was triumphant. "Lived only for you. Sacrificed my life for you. You need me, Rodrigo. I'm the only one who can protect you from everything. From pain. From loss."

Rodrigo lifted his head.

"I don't want to be protected. Not anymore. I never wanted you to do any of this," he said in a low voice. "I'm sorry, Marnie. It's time for you to go."

She looked flummoxed. "Go!"

"I'm in love with my wife. Because of you…"

Because of you, I've betrayed her, he almost said. But

that wasn't fair. It hadn't just been Marnie's lies that kept him from loving Lola. He'd been scared. Scared of losing control. Scared of abandonment and pain. Taking a deep breath, he said quietly, "It's time for you to find another job and a different man to love."

His assistant's face crumpled. "No!" she cried. "I don't know how to do anything else." She gave a sob, wrapping her arms around herself. "I don't know how to change."

He hadn't either, Rodrigo realized. He might have spent the rest of his life focusing only on wealth and power, unloved and dead inside, as lonely as a mummy in a tomb full of cold treasures.

If not for Lola's warmth. Her bravery. Her love.

Because of her, he had the chance to be better. To make better choices. To be brave enough to change.

"I'm sorry," Rodrigo said, looking down at his assistant. He lifted the duffel bag with the change of clothes back to his shoulder. "You'll get severance for your years of service. But I love my wife. You have to know you can't work for me anymore."

Marnie wiped her eyes. "Then what will I do?"

"I don't know." Turning away, he paused to look back at the door. "I hear Sergei Morozov is moving back to Moscow and looking for a new assistant."

She blinked at him, looking like a mole who's just seen the sun.

"Good luck," he said.

Turning away, Rodrigo strode through his office, yelling right and left for everyone to go home, to spend the holiday with their families and friends. His employees' eyes lit up with delight. But he couldn't wait. He nearly ran out of the walnut-paneled lobby, holding his phone to his ear, telling his pilot to get the plane ready.

He had to see Lola. Tonight. Before the New Year began. He'd be brave enough to tell her he loved her.

But as he jumped into his car and stomped down hard on the gas, driving down the sunlit highway toward the airport, Rodrigo wondered if he'd be too late.

CHAPTER ELEVEN

WHY, OH, WHY had Lola ever let her friends talk her into this?

"It's almost time!" Hallie crowed, kissing her husband passionately in the crowded rooftop restaurant. "Just ten minutes left!"

All around Lola, happy couples were counting down the minutes until the start of a new year. Nearby, she saw Stefano kissing Tess under the mistletoe.

They were also celebrating Cristiano Moretti's new acquisition of this building, an old, rundown chain hotel with a location overlooking Times Square. He'd closed on the hotel yesterday. Tomorrow, the vast remodeling project would begin, to bring the property into line with the high standards of his luxury Campania hotel brand.

Only the rooftop restaurant was still open, with its Art Deco–style bar and enormous windows and terrace overlooking Times Square; and it was only open to Cristiano's closest family and friends, for his glamorous black tie New Year's Eve party. Everyone was drinking champagne and ogling the bright lights and electronic billboards of Times Square, shining brightly and shimmering in the cold winter's night below, as they, and about a million people on the streets, waited for the magical moment when the ball would drop, and a new year would begin.

But Lola just felt sad.

She shivered in the silvery, sparkly dress she'd borrowed from Hallie. Her friends were worried about her. Since she and Jett had arrived from Los Angeles last week, they'd complained that Lola didn't seem like her old self. She didn't brashly give her opinion. She didn't boss anyone around. Even spending Christmas Day with her little sisters and their parents, as wonderful as they'd been, hadn't healed her broken heart. Though Kelsey and Johanna would always be her sisters, she missed Rodrigo. She missed her husband. She wanted him.

Her heart felt broken.

Lola looked down at her palm. She held the plain gold wedding band she'd had engraved for him. The ring she'd meant to give him for Christmas. She'd brought it with her tonight, telling herself that she'd toss it away at midnight and start the new year fresh.

But feeling it in her hand, she couldn't let it go.

Oh, if he had only loved her!

Wiping a tear savagely before anyone could see it, she left the bar and went out onto the rooftop terrace. It was very cold, but the frigid, numbing air was a relief against her hot skin. It was also a relief to get away from her friends.

Hallie and Tess kept giving her worried looks, trying to tempt her to eat from the appetizer trays. They'd bullied her into coming tonight. Even the fact that she'd given in— meekly, without a fight—had seemed to worry them. She could still see them peeking at her through the windows, even as they danced in the arms of their adoring husbands.

Lola felt hollowed out.

She was glad for Tess and Hallie. She truly was. But they'd risked everything for love, and won.

Lola had risked everything, and lost.

A lump rose in her throat. *Stop it*, she told herself furiously, hating her self-pity. She was lucky. Her son was healthy and well. She had custody. Her baby sisters were back in her life. She had good friends. She had a place to live, at the Morettis' large, comfortable home in the West Village, where Jett was now being watched by their long-time nanny, along with Hallie's baby, Jack.

She'd even been offered two different jobs, one in Cristiano's hotel business, the other in Tess's growing fashion company.

Lola had refused both. She'd told her friends she intended to go to community college, and maybe even law school. They'd loved that idea. So did she. It was Rodrigo who'd given it to her. In that sense, he'd believed in her, in a way no one else ever had.

But for now, she couldn't think of the future. She still had money saved. She'd think of it all later.

She looked down at the diamond Rodrigo had given her, sparkling on her left hand. She should send it back, she knew, like she'd sent back the necklace. But as heavy and cold as the ring was, she hadn't been able to take it off.

Their divorce would be simple, at least. All the details had been arranged in the prenup. Any day now, she expected to get the paperwork from Rodrigo's lawyers. Lola looked out at Times Square gleaming around her. She was lucky, she thought dully. It all would be easy. Happy New Year.

Enough, she told herself savagely. *Go back to the party. Pretend you're having a good time, for your friends' sake, if not your own.*

Wiping her eyes one last time, she forced her face into a smile and turned around. Then she stopped with an intake of breath.

There, standing in front of her, was Rodrigo.

Lola's legs went weak.

"What are you doing here?" she whispered, wondering if he was a dream wrought by her feverish heart.

Rodrigo's chiseled face was darkly handsome beneath

the bright lights of Times Square as he came toward Lola on the rooftop terrace. He was dressed in a black shirt and trousers beneath a black overcoat. His jawline was dark with a five o'clock shadow. His voice was low and deep. "I came for you."

He was real. He had to be. She could see the white cloud of his breath in the cold air. And she'd never seen anything so beautiful in her life.

Shaking, Lola took a step forward. Reaching up, she put her hand against his rough cheek. She felt him tremble beneath her touch. Just like she was trembling.

There were shadows beneath his eyes. As if he hadn't slept all week, any more than she had. "For me?"

Rodrigo put his hand over her own. "I came to tell you that you were right."

Lola's hopes, which had been rising as high as the Empire State Building, crashed to the ground.

"You mean about Marnie. I was right about her."

"Not just her." His dark eyes searched hers. "About everything."

"What are you saying?" she asked breathlessly.

Slowly, Rodrigo pulled her into his arms. His body felt so powerful. So solid. So strong. And so were his black eyes as he looked down at her.

"I'm in love with you, Lola."

Her heart stopped in her chest. "What?"

"I've always loved you." Gently, he moved his hands down her hair, against the bare skin of her shoulders above her party dress. "I loved you so much, it scared the hell out of me. Because I knew I'd someday lose you, just like I lost the others." He paused. "But now…"

"Now?" she choked out, searching his gaze.

"I'm not scared anymore." Rodrigo looked down at her, giving her a smile that seemed lit up from within. "After you left, everything fell apart. And I realized nothing else matters. You're all I want. All I need. You're everything. Because I love you."

As she stared at him, her heart twisted in her chest.

"And I was a fool." Rodrigo searched her gaze fiercely. "Marnie might have sabotaged those other relationships, but so did I."

"You?"

"The moment they agreed to marry me, I became restless, wanting to be away from them. But with you, it was different. With you… I admire you. Respect you. You're not just my lover. You're my friend. My partner."

As if from a million miles away, she heard noise from the party, as someone shouted, "The countdown has begun!"

"All I want is to be with you," he whispered. "Forever and always." His hand tightened against her shoulder. "You're my soul mate."

"Twenty…"

"And I know I ruined everything," Rodrigo said. "Leaving you like that, kicking you out of my car just for telling me the truth…" He shuddered. "You don't know how much I wish I could go back. But all I can do is go forward. And hope you'll forgive me. Tell me," he whispered, running his hands through her hair. "How I can win you back…"

"Ten…"

Lola stared at him, too overcome with emotion to speak.

His expression fell. Then his jaw set as his eyes narrowed with determination. "I'll do whatever it takes to win you back, Lola. Anything. Even if it takes everything I possess. Even if it takes the rest of my life—"

"Stop." Trembling, she reached her finger to his lips. They felt soft and sensual, warm to the touch. A shiver of desire went through her.

"Five…"

Opening her hand, she held out the golden wedding band on her palm. "This is my answer."

Emotion was raw on his face as he took the ring. Then he saw the inscription: *I love you now and always.*

Rodrigo looked up with an intake of breath.

"One! Happy New Year!"

A growl came from the back of his throat, and he pulled her into his powerful arms, wrapping her tight. And lowering his head, he kissed Lola as she'd never been kissed before: with pure, heartfelt love, holding nothing back. She returned his kiss, with the same promise and need.

They were fated. Bound. Married.

Soul mates.

A cheer rose up behind them, yanking Lola out of her spell. Pressing her cheek against his chest, she saw the Morettis and Zaccos and all the rest of the party pressed against the restaurant's double-height windows, grinning and applauding. Hallie and Tess were giving her beaming smiles and holding up champagne glasses, as if they'd always known love would win.

And it was true, Lola thought with tears in her eyes. Love won. No matter how difficult and awful life could be, no matter how much grief and pain a person endured, love could always win.

"Let's live in New York," he murmured suddenly.

She looked up at him joyfully. "Are you serious?"

"Why not?" He gave her a sudden wicked grin. "I hear it's 'a hotbed of media companies that will dominate the future of the entertainment business.'"

She giggled. "Not to mention it's near all our family and friends."

"Yes. Not to mention that." Rodrigo's face grew serious. "I've realized whatever makes you happy, makes me happy, too." Sliding the golden band on his left ring finger, he cupped her face in his hands. "I've spent my whole life looking for you, *querida*," he said huskily, looking down at her with tears shining in his black eyes. "And now I've found you, I'm never going to let you go."

"I love you," Lola whispered, smiling through her own tears.

"I love you. Now and forever." And as Rodrigo lowered his lips to hers, they started the new year, their new lives, with a kiss she'd never forget.

Summer had come to New York at last. The trees were green, the sun was shining and the tourists were in full bloom, returning to the city with the faithful constancy of the swallows of San Juan Capistrano.

Three friends were giggling together in the spacious, flower-filled backyard of a West Village mansion, watching as their three billionaire husbands argued loudly about the best method of barbecuing steaks.

"They'll get it eventually," Hallie said, smiling as she gave her fifteen-month-old baby, Jack, his favorite toy shovel before he toddled off to dig in the sunny garden.

"Oh, yes," agreed Tess, playing patty-cake with sixteen-month-old Esme, before the baby toddled unsteadily after Jack.

Looking at her friends in disbelief, Lola cuddled the youngest baby, eleven-month-old Jett, who was sleeping in her arms. "We might have to order pizza."

The three women giggled, then hid their smiles as the men looked over with a suspicious glare.

Taking a sip of sparkling water, Hallie sobered as she tilted her head back to look over her magnificent private garden, rare for Manhattan, and the four-story brick townhouse, at her toddler digging up flowers and her husband practically getting into a fistfight with his best friends over the best use of marinade.

"Can you believe how much has changed since we all first met at the single moms' group?" she said. Tilting her head, she said softly, "This time last year, I was desperate and alone."

"We all were," said Lola.

"I thought I'd never have what I wanted most." Tears rose to Hallie's eyes. "A family. A home."

"And I wanted love," Tess said, a dreamy smile tracing her lips. "Love that would last forever."

"I was the only one who was practical," Lola grumbled. "Unlike you two numbskulls, I knew money made the world go 'round."

The other two stared at her, then burst into a laugh.

"What?" Lola said, looking between them indignantly.

"You can't fool us," chided Tess, still snickering.

"Yeah, Lola. The jig is up."

"What are you talking about?"

"You never wanted money, you old softie." Hallie grinned. "You wanted family and home and love, like the rest of us."

"Don't worry," Tess said, patting her hand. "Your secret's safe with us."

For a moment, Lola looked disgruntled. Then she sighed, leaning back in the comfortable patio chair, as she reached for her own glass of sparkling water with lemon. "All right," she said softly. She smiled at them. "You got me. That was what I really wanted, all along."

Tess squeezed her hand, and then all three women leaned back in their chairs, relishing the warmth of the June afternoon, sipping identical drinks, as they watched their husbands argue over the best way to barbecue and their babies play in the sunshine.

Flashing the husbands a guilty glance, Hallie whispered, "Can you keep a secret?"

"We have no secrets now," said Lola, waving her glass airily.

"Tell us," Tess begged.

Hallie blushed, then she looked up with a smile so bright, her brown eyes glowed. "There's a reason I'm drinking sparkling water tonight, instead of sangria."

"Me, too," breathed Tess.

Lola sat up straight in her chair. "Me, too."

The three women stared at each other, wide-eyed.

"All of us together—"

"Pregnant again—"

"Friends forever—"

And in a loud burst of noise, they all hugged each other in a raucous cacophony of laughter and tears.

On the other side of the garden, the three men frowned, looking across the yard at their wives.

"I wonder what that's all about," said Cristiano.

"Could they be talking about us?" wondered Prince Stefano.

"Doubtful," said Rodrigo. While the other two men were distracted, he took the opportunity to commandeer the grill. Let the Italians stick to pasta, he thought. Only Spaniards knew *parrillada*. And he knew Lola liked her steaks spicy, like her man. Like her life.

"What could make them cheer like that?" Cristiano pondered.

"Yes, what?" Stefano frowned.

Rodrigo looked back over his shoulder, at the sunlit garden, their happy children, their mysterious, powerful, beautiful wives. And he flashed a grin back at the other men. "Something tells me we'll soon find out."

* * * * *

COMING SOON!

We really hope you enjoyed reading this book. If you're looking for more romance, be sure to head to the shops when new books are available on

Thursday 15th November

To see which titles are coming soon, please visit
millsandboon.co.uk

MILLS & BOON

MILLS & BOON

Coming next month

MARRIED FOR HIS ONE-NIGHT HEIR
Jennifer Hayward

'What were you going to tell Leo when the time came? The truth? Or were you going to tell him that his father was a high-priced thug?'

She flinched. Lifted a fluttering hand to her throat. 'I hadn't thought that far ahead,' she admitted. 'We've been too busy trying to survive. Making a life for ourselves. Leo's welfare has been my top priority.'

Which he believed. It was the only reason he wasn't going to take his child and walk. Do to her exactly what she'd done to him. Because as angry as he was, as unforgivable as what she had done had been, he had to take the situation she'd been in into account. It had taken guts for her to walk away from her life. Courage. She'd put Leo first, something his own mother hadn't done. And she had been young and scared. All things he couldn't ignore.

Gia set her gaze on his, apprehension flaring in her eyes. 'I can't change the past, Santo, the decisions I made. But I can make this right. Clearly,' she acknowledged, 'you are going to want to be a part of Leo's life. I was thinking about solutions last night. I thought you could visit us here... Get Leo used to the idea of having you around, and then, when he is older, more able to understand the situation, we can tell him the truth.'

A slow curl of heat unraveled inside of him, firing the blood in his veins to dangerously combustible levels. 'And what do you propose we tell him when I visit? That I am that *friend* you referred to the other night? How many *friends* do you have, Gia?'

Her face froze. 'I have been building a *life* here. Establishing a career. There has been no time for dating. All I do is work and spend time with Leo, who is a handful as you can imagine, as all three-year-olds tend to be.'

The defensively issued words lodged themselves in his throat. 'I can't actually imagine,' he said softly, 'because you've deprived me of the right to know that, Gia. You have deprived me of *everything*.'

She blanched. He set down his glass on the bar. 'I am his *father*. I have missed three years of his life. You think a *weekend pass* is going to suffice? A few dips in the sea as he learns to swim?' He shook his head. 'I want *every day* with him. I want to wake up with him bouncing on the bed. I want to take him to the park and throw a ball around. I want to hear about his day when I tuck him into bed. I want it *all*.'

'What else can we do?' she queried helplessly. 'You live in New York and I live here. Leo is settled and happy. A limited custody arrangement is the only realistic solution for us.'

'It is *not* a viable proposition.' His low growl made her jump. 'That's not how this is going to work, Gia.'

She eyed him warily. 'Which part?'

'All of it. I have a proposal for you. It's the only one on the table. Nonnegotiable on all points. Take it or leave it.'

The wariness written across her face intensified. 'Which is?'

'We do what's in the best interests of our child. You marry me, we create a life together in New York and give Leo the family he deserves.'

Continue reading
MARRIED FOR HIS ONE-NIGHT HEIR
Jennifer Hayward

www.millsandboon.co.uk

Copyright ©2018 by Jennifer Hayward

LET'S TALK
Romance

For exclusive extracts, competitions
and special offers, find us online:

f facebook.com/millsandboon

🐦 @MillsandBoon

📷 @MillsandBoonUK

Get in touch on 01413 063232

For all the latest titles coming soon, visit
millsandboon.co.uk/nextmonth

Want even more ROMANCE?

Join our bookclub today!

'Mills & Boon books, the perfect way to escape for an hour or so.'

Miss W. Dyer

'Excellent service, promptly delivered and very good subscription choices.'

Miss A. Pearson

'You get fantastic special offers and the chance to get books before they hit the shops'

Mrs V. Hall

Visit millsandbook.co.uk/Bookclub

and save on brand new books.

MILLS & BOON